Diary of a Demonologist

By Darla Broadwater

Version 1.0

ISBN: 978-0-9855790-2-9

To Eric, who has patiently listened to all of my stories and come up with a few of his own.

From the author: This book has been a long time in the making. There have been many obstacles along the way, like someone, or something, did not want it out there. You see, this book has spiritual overtones as it was written by a Christian author. Yes, it has references to the Bible and the Lord. After all, God is the author of my talent. No, it is not preachy. You don't have to believe in anything at all to enjoy this book.

There have even been missing things along the way- a thumb drive that was mysteriously erased with no trace at all of the writing that it contained.

I hope you enjoy reading this book as much as it was an adventure for me to create and re-create it!

Darla

Entry One- Disappearance

PART I- CHAPTER ONE

Sometimes selfishness takes on a life of its own…

"Well, fine, I'll just get the money somewhere else then!" Denni Selwood snapped, slamming down the receiver of her neon blue phone. She leaned back against her black formica bar and let out a long, harsh sigh- one that shook her entire skinny body.

"I don't understand it", she said out loud to herself. "All I've done for that girl and she can't give me a lousy fifty!! I'm going to have to find out why she's being such a witch! She probably has her boyfriend rammed up her crack and has to ask his *permission* first!"

The "girl" was Denni's best friend, or who she *thought* was her best friend, Annabella Wilshur. They had known each other since the third grade and since then, nothing could keep them apart. They had shared everything; including on one occasion, each other's boyfriends. But, that incident was quickly passed over and filed away in the back of their minds, like clothes that you want to wear but can't fit into any longer. It gnaws at you but you *try* not to think about it. It's just better that way. This past year, however, they had started to grow apart. Her and Annabella rarely talked anymore and when they did, Annabella always had an excuse as to why she had to hurry up and get off the phone.

Denni sauntered over to her black leather couch and sat down. She really needed the fifty dollars today, too. A forlorn look crossed her face. She had a utility bill to pay, but since she didn't get the fifty bucks… She had a dealer to pay too, and that was more important. Her last three hundred was going to go to him. She had that money already spent, and nothing was going to intrude on *her* buying what *she* wanted, which in this case was heroin.

That's OK; she didn't need too much food this week. Good thing she had some soups in the pantry and a few apples in the fridge.

It wasn't *her* fault that the gas and electric rates were so high. She couldn't help it that the CEOs of these companies were soooooooo hoggy. It wasn't *her* fault that her power was going to get turned off if she didn't pay. There were just some things she needed, and it wasn't her fault that Annabella wouldn't lend her the money and that Denni herself didn't make enough.

Which reminded her, today was Sunday and she had to go to work tomorrow. She hated her job. Being a secretary at a law firm was not gravy. There were so many demands on her time, all day long. She was lucky if she had enough time to go to the bathroom. Denni did not realize the fact that in this day and age, she should be thankful she had a job; and in all actuality, a good-paying one. The law firm was very secure and had a lot of clients. Denni had been there for ten years now and had worked her way up to being the secretary of the second to the top lawyer. She had also worked her way up to making $30.87 an hour with more raises to go. So what if hardly anyone liked her at work? It wasn't *her* fault she had something to complain about all the time. She just had a harder life than everyone else.

She slouched down further in her plush leather couch and crossed her arms.

"I need to think", she whispered out loud. "*Think!*"

She grabbed her telephone book and started searching for more numbers; more people that might feel sorry for her. She stopped at the number of another one of her good friends, who this time happened to be a guy. Maybe she would have better luck with him. She knew he had the hots for her for a very long time now, and they could always take it out in trade.

She thought it was more than fair since she was worth a whole lot more than fifty dollars, anyway.

She dialed the number. It rang four times. "C'mon, *answer*!!" She said impatiently. "You need an *answering* machine!"

"Hello?" A male voice said groggily after the seventh ring.

"Gary, what are you doing?"

"Oh hey, Denni, I was taking a nap", he answered, still drunk from sleep. "I was bored."

"Well… how about coming over here for a while?" Denni's voice got softer with every word. She knew the answer before she even got all of the words out.

"OK… let me take a shower and I'll be right over."

"Don't worry about a shower." She hung up.

She knew he'd be over in about fifteen minutes, so she went ahead and put some fresh towels and soap in the bathroom. They'd be needing these. She briefly checked her appearance in the mirror. "Not bad", she said, cocking one bony hip to the side and putting her skeletal hand on it. Yeah, it wasn't too bad… for an addict.

Just then, the doorbell rang; Gary had arrived.

"Wow, only seven minutes!" Denni exclaimed after checking the clock, and after opening the door she said, "You must have flown over here."

"Well, you sounded like you were in need."

"You're right, Gary, *both* of us are", Denni replied, putting her arms around his waist and smiling.

He suddenly pushed her away with such a force that sent her reeling back to the couch where she plopped down with a *"whissshhh"*, a puff of air making her black hair fly upwards.

"So, why all of a sudden?!"

Denni just sat there staring at him with her mouth open. She tried to look shocked and innocent.

"What do you mean? You always come over here."

Gary was giving her a baleful look, the look a dog might give his master before he bites him. "You know full well what I mean. You've pushed my advances under the rug all of these years, and now all of a sudden-"

Denni cut him off. "Gary, I've always been attracted to you." That was a complete lie because honestly, she didn't see anything attractive about him at all. In fact, she wouldn't even wipe her floors up with him.

"I've just been afraid that getting involved on a different level would affect the great friendship that we have." This statement was entirely true. She knew that friendships were never quite the same if they lasted at all; *especially* if the break-up was not mutual.

"Oh, I'm sure it won't", Gary replied with a serious look on his face. *He really cares about me*, Denni thought ruefully. *Too bad I don't care about him that much. Oh well, I've got to do what I've got to do.*

She looked in the direction of the bathroom and then smiled up at him. "Let's shower, shall we?"

"I'd rather take a bath." He had a huge smile on his plain, if not unique, face. His brown eyes were sparkling with anticipation. "Is your tub big enough for the both of us?"

"I'm sure." She gave him a smile that was equally large, if not larger, but inside, she was retching. *Wow, I sure am good!* She thought. *After all, money talks...*

They walked towards the direction of the bathroom.

TWO

Afterwards, Denni was left sitting on her leather couch. Alone. Gary had wanted to stay, but said he didn't want to "rush right into things". It was just as well; she hadn't planned on him spending the night, anyway.

She'd gotten what she wanted, just like always. Only this time, she had to use her body to get it. Or should she say, *Gary* had to use her body. It kind of hurt for her to sit down. Gary hadn't wanted to "rush right into things", but he'd wanted to have sex alright. Denni had been obliged to not only go through with it once, but twice. She felt used and dirty for the first time in her life. It was a good thing he didn't feel the need for any obligatory extras that usually come with the main dish.

On the flip side, it kind of felt good to do it without any emotional attachment whatsoever outside of friendship. Even though she felt emptier than ever from the experience (not to mention disgusted), at least she knew that *her* feelings weren't going to be hurt. And that was all that mattered.

While Denni was sitting there with her head in her hands pondering all of this, she felt another thing as well: the feeling of a presence in the room. It wasn't a very strong one, but it was there all the same, like a faint odor that you can detect but you can't *quite* put your finger on what it is.

Maybe Gary was thinking about her. She knew he did all of the time. They probably had that mind communication thing going. Yeah, that's what it was.

She picked up the fifty he'd left her on the table and rubbed it between her fingers for a few minutes. It was a very good feeling to her- money in her hand. She wondered how long that feeling would last. If things stayed the same as they'd been… it wouldn't be but a day; maybe even a few hours.

She rose up off of the couch, clutching the money tightly in her hand. She started for her coat hanging on the back of one of her dining room chairs, and then stopped. She had planned on leaving right this minute, going down to the library, getting on the computer, and paying her gas and electric bill. But, she thought the better of it. Forget them.

They could wait another day, or for that matter, another month. She'd only be that much behind. She could make it up one way or another. Times were tough. She just had too many other bills to pay, and important ones at that. If they decided to shut her utilities off in the meantime… so be it. She had plenty of candles, and she could *make* her own heat. It wasn't her fault the utility rates were so outrageous.

She picked up the phone and dialed another one of her old friends- another guy. She hadn't had coke in a long, long time and kind of missed it. The phone was answered on the second ring.

"Hello, Jim? How are you?" She asked sweetly. "I was wondering if you'd be able to do me a favor…"

THREE

It had only been two hours since Gary was over, so Denni was busily tidying up the bathroom. She felt she needed another shower after being with him, even though she didn't sweat that much.

One good thing: she liked Jim a whole lot better. She just didn't know if he liked her in that way or not. Well, even if he didn't, she sure was going to try. Besides, she had to thank him properly. After all, he *was* doing her a favor by cutting her such a good deal. For that, she'd be forever grateful. *Especially* now that she'd fallen on such hard times as these.

She padded out of the bathroom to get some bubble bath out of the hall closet. There was none.

"That's funny", she said to herself, "I just got some three days ago." It was strawberry scented, her favorite. She had went into a dollar store where everything actually was a dollar and picked up some things that she needed- bubble bath being one of them. She knew she'd put it in this closet, and exactly where in this closet, and nobody else had been in there but her.

"Man!" She exclaimed as she started pulling things off the shelves and throwing them on the floor.

She finally decided to give up once she had torn the whole thing apart. She knew it wouldn't be long until Jim would be at the door.

Oh well. They would just have to settle for soap, and there was only one bar of that left. She *knew* she had more of that. It couldn't be used for anything else, for Pete's sake.

Just as she was carefully arranging everything in key places around the bathroom, there was a knock at the door. From the way it sounded, the person on the other side must have been impatient or aggravated. Denni figured the first one. Jim never liked to wait around anywhere for too long and besides, he probably had it figured out what Denni had in store for him.

She checked her reflection in the mirror for the second time that day, flipping her medium-length black hair back. Her hair used to be so shiny it was blinding, but now it was starting to lose its luster. She could blame half of that on her addiction, the other half on bad nutrition. A plain, dull face stared back, light brown eyes a little bloodshot and glassy, but to Denni, it was one of the most beautiful female faces in the world. At least *she* always thought it was. That's all that mattered, wasn't it?

"I can't stay long", Jim said rather breathlessly as Denni opened the door and he brushed past her. She was clad in a thin white tank top (no bra), and short dark blue cotton shorts.

She eyed him curiously. "Why not? You don't have some time to talk to me?"

"No, not today. I've got some business to take care of."

Denni knew what Jim's "business" was. She was hoping that it could wait for her to do what she had to do. If not...

She slowly sidled up to him; one of those slow, sexy walks that a woman does when she's either trying to seduce a man or to get him to do what she wants. The effect, and sometimes the cause, was always the same.

She put her hands on his shoulders, and pressed her stomach hard against his.

"C'mon, baby, wouldn't you like to stay awhile and talk to me?" She asked softly while looking up at him through her lashes.

Jim pushed her away. "Denni, what has gotten into you?? You never worried if I stayed before." He looked and sounded a bit irritated. Deep down, he was thinking that she was starting to act like one of those "coke whores" he always dealt with, and that disgusted him.

"I'm lonely, Jim", was the sultry reply. "Please, stay and keep me company." She grabbed him to her and now her arms were wrapped tightly around his waist, her pelvis grinding into his.

Denni knew what was going to happen before Jim even thought of it: he was starting to become aroused. No matter how hard he tried, (and he was trying very hard-he pushed her away again), there was no denying the stiffness that was making itself known in the front of his jeans. It was good to be needed. Despite his cool exterior, Jim was no different than most men. And Denni knew, like most men, he didn't like to let a good hard-on go to waste.

"So", she said softly.

Jim stood there staring at her, a dumbfounded look on his face. Denni guessed one more push would do the trick.

"Are you ready?"

She was right: Jim followed her lead into the bedroom.

FOUR

"I'll call you tonight. Do you think maybe we can get together again sometime tomorrow?"

Denni knew what Jim's "get together" meant: another replay of today's acrobatics. Still, she was looking forward to it. She had a lot of fun with him, and maybe he could bring her some more "goodies".

"Sure, baby, why not?" Her tone was dripping with honey, but she'd tried to keep her enthusiasm down a few notches. Didn't want to get his ego *too* far out there.

Denni chuckled to herself as she closed the door behind Jim. She'd put on her *best* performance today. There was no holding back for her or him, and as a result, she had gotten her coke for free. So, she was fifty dollars to the good, and at that price she was stealing it. *But still,* she thought, *if I can get out of paying even fifty dollars I'm gonna do it!*

She laughed then; long and hard. It got to the point where it was so bad, she flopped on the couch clutching her stomach, tears streaming down her face. That was when she looked up, and saw her black formica bar missing.

PART II- CHAPTER ONE

Denni looked at the clock for what must have been the twentieth time so far. One in the afternoon. She let out a long heaving sigh. Four hours yet to go. She didn't know how she was going to do it- not many people had called, and she was totally caught up on paperwork. It was a very slow day, one of many lately, which up to this point had been unusual for this law firm. She guessed with the economy the way it was, people were trying to stay out of situations where they needed lawyers, unless it was to claim bankruptcy.

She got up and crossed the floor towards the other offices. It was time to do a little visiting with her friends; some of the other secretaries who worked there. She hadn't used up all of her resources at the firm- yet.

She peeked in at her friend Sophie who worked for the top lawyer there - one of the founding partners. One day Denni hoped to be in Sophie's shoes, and likewise in Dan Zimmerman's bed. He and his secretary had been carrying on for well over two years now. Sophie as a rule was pretty well taken care of. Denni hoped that it would stay that way and that nothing ever happened that would mean Sophie's job. But if it did, well… even though they were the best of friends, Denni would be more than happy to take over.

Sophie looked up from her desk, an instant smile spreading across her pretty face.

"Hi, Denni! How's it going?" She looked around and lowered her voice. "How was your weekend?"

One of the secretaries (her name was Joy Gorley) that sat outside of Sophie's office was always listening, and would frequently get up from her desk to come and join in the conversation, uninvited. Not only would she join the conversation, but she would offer her take on why things would be going wrong for Denni or Sophie, and if they would just start going to church…

A bible passage or two would always be quoted, and usually she would tell them upon leaving that they needed to turn their lives over to the Lord. Sophie knew that Joy would be in her office in a minute upon hearing of the weekend's festivities. Neither she nor Denni were in the mood to entertain her today.

Sophie, without giving Denni a chance to answer her question went on, "My weekend was great, as usual. Dan took me out on the lake all day Saturday." Her voice took on a hushed, almost reverent tone at this last statement.

"Me and Jim got together for a few hours last night."

Sophie knew exactly what happened. Her eyes widened. "Oh?! Your friend Jim?! He's *really cute!*" She had seen him on a few occasions when Denni had parties, and all she knew what that he was a friend- not Denni's dealer as well.

"Yeah, I think so too." Denni wasn't going to tell her about Gary, no matter how close her and Sophie were.

"I bet you're on cloud nine! What was he like?" Her voice was still lowered, lest Joy come running around the corner.

"What do you think I do, sleep with everyone whenever I get a chance?" Denni tried her best to look appalled.

Sophie frowned. "Yes. I *know* how bad you wanted him. All of this talk about 'I want to take our friendship to new heights' and all of that. So cut it out and tell me everything." She leaned a little farther over her desk.

"Well, you know…" Denni rolled her eyes innocently enough.

"So you *did* do it!! I *knew* it! You can't fool me one bit!" Sophie jumped up and down in quick excited motions in her seat, her short wavy blonde hair bouncing along with her. Then, with a smile on her face, "So what's he like? Give me *all* of the gory details."

"He was great, Sophie, just great. I think that's all I am going to say."

Both Sophie and Denni snickered at that one, even more so when out of the corners of their eyes they saw Joy get up and peek around the door of Sophie's office. She did not come any further, much to their relief.

Sophie then gave Denni a look and a smile that said, 'Please do go on.'

Denni did.

When she finished telling Sophie everything, she smiled and winked at her and then walked back to her desk. She looked at the clock again. Two-thirty! She sighed in partial relief. Talking with Sophie was always a great way to make the time fly.

A frown then briefly passed over her face as she had another thought. She was very disturbed about her bar missing. There was no way that it could have happened. *I have got to be hallucinating*, she thought. *It must be the DTs for whatever reason.*

For one thing, she had been home the entire weekend. Also, there was no evidence whatsoever of forced entry. And the last and most confusing point of all was the fact that her bar was still right there *before* Jim had come over!! She knew this for a fact, because she had made herself a drink. And as far as Jim being a suspect… that was impossible. She had seen him out. Besides, how could you carry away someone's bar singlehandedly, *especially* without them noticing??

As far as she was concerned, reporting this to the police was a total waste of time. They would probably end up taking her to the Baltimore County Center for Behavioral and Psychiatric Disorders, unless they tested her for drugs first. Not only that, they probably would try to lock her up for insurance fraud. Any way you looked at it, she would not win.

Sophie then passed by her desk. "You must really have plans for tonight", she said in her sing-song voice.

"Huh…? What do you mean?" Denni was in a daze.

"It's the time you've been waiting for all day. I can't believe you're not ready. I'd wait for you, but I have to get a head start on *my* plans for tonight. See you tomorrow."

"See you, Sophie." Wow- it *was* five o'clock!
Time flies when you're confused.

TWO

A smile was on Denni's lips as she strode through her apartment door. *I'll just get me a shower, grab a small bite to eat…* she thought, except there wasn't anything *to* eat. She didn't go to the store today. Not that she had that much money *to* go, anyway.

She walked across the room to get the phone and dial Jim's number. It was on the floor where the bar used to be. *I'll just have to move it over on the table next to the couch*, she thought, as she spun around to face it, waiting for him to answer; handset clutched tightly in one hand, her keys in the other.

Then, both of them hit the floor just as Jim picked up. There was a muted "…Hello?" on the other end.

"Oh no *WAY*!!!" Denni screamed. "No *WAY*!!!"

Again, "…Hello? Hello? Is that you, Denni?"

She came to her senses just for a split second and snatched up the phone.

"I'm sorry, Jim."

"Hey, what's going *on* over there?"

"There's been a bit of a mishap. Are you coming over tonight?"

"Yeah, when?"

"Whenever you're ready, honey. I'm just going to grab a quick shower. Do you want anything to eat?" If he did, they would just have to go out, or have it delivered. She didn't have any dinner supplies.

"Yeah, I'll take something."

"OK, I guess we can decide what we want when you get here." Her voice was slightly shaken, slightly on edge.

"Denni, are you OK?"

"Yeah, I'm alright", she lied.

"Somehow, I'm not convinced. I'll be over in about fifteen minutes." Click. He had hung up.

########

Exactly fifteen minutes later, Denni was freshly showered and dressed in faded jeans and a black t-shirt, and Jim was knocking at her door.

"Hey, what happened to your furniture?!" He exclaimed while walking through the door. His face then took on a look of disbelief. "Hey, you didn't…"

She cut him short. "No, Jim, I didn't sell it. *Especially* since I can't afford to be without it or buy more later. The bar was missing last night, the sofa and table when I got home today."

"Did somebody break in?"

"Look around you, Jim. There are no signs anywhere of forced entry." She smiled inwardly to herself in spite of this- she sounded like a detective.

He went over to the door and inspected it, trying to see anything at all. Like he didn't believe her; like she didn't know what forced entry was. She started to feel her cheeks getting hot.

"Yeah, you're right. No broken windows either?" Didn't he think she would have called the cops if she saw any?

"I don't think anyone would climb all the way up to the third floor, Jim." A small amount of irritation entered her voice.

"You'd be surprised. Do you think that maybe the apartment manager or maintenance might have been in here?"

That *was* a possibility. "I was thinking about that", she said with a thoughtful look on her face. "But maintenance is not supposed to go into anyone's apartment without prior notice, and usually, it is at the renter's request. Besides, at least three people would have to come in here to take that bar away. Which reminds me!" She snapped her fingers. Jim looked at her quizzically.

"I forgot to mention that there is *no way* anyone could have come in here and taken my bar. It was here when you came over last night, right?"

"Yes, it was."

"Well, after you left is when I discovered it missing."

A frown came over Jim's handsome face, knitting his perfectly groomed brows together. "You've got to be kidding."

"No, I wish I was. I couldn't believe my own eyes at first. But after I knew for sure that it was *not* a hallucination… man, I think I need to get off the drugs."

"Hmmm… I don't know what to tell you, Denni. Sounds like something supernatural to me." Denni couldn't believe Jim was actually saying something stupid like that, but when she thought about it, it really couldn't be anything else.

"That's the only real reasonable explanation I can think of. Just keep an eye out for anything that grows legs while you're over here for me, OK?"

He pulled her towards him and gave her a kiss. "Sure will. Now how about a snack before dinner?" He smiled as he proffered a medium-sized bag of coke.

"No thanks. I think I just gave it up."

#########

Jim was already gone by the time Denni got up for work at seven-thirty. He had left her a note tacked to his pillow, though. It said, 'Talk to you later tonight. Love Jim.' She smiled. It was a start. He had never left her anything before, and if he did write something, it certainly didn't say 'Love Jim' on it. Her smile broadened. She felt a little better already. No, it was more than feeling better. Her whole outlook on things was brighter now.

But it didn't stay that way for long. She walked into the kitchen to grab something to eat and ended up passed out on the floor.

# # # # # # # #

It was some time before she awoke; maybe about a half hour. She looked dazedly around her, wondering just where she was. Then, she remembered.

She had come in here to get some breakfast, and upon opening the refrigerator, saw that there was none. It was empty. Everything gone. She frantically searched all of her cabinets and they were all cleared out too. Even her dishes and silverware were missing; including those in the dishwasher and counter drain, and even right down to the spoon she had left on the stove from her noodles.

"Now I *know* I'm not going crazy!!" She yelled aloud. "This is *ridiculous*!! Who in the *world* would steal food and dishes?? I can't *believe* this!! I can't afford to buy more this week!" She whined.

Then she remembered the fifty dollars that she had. Frantic, she turned around out of the kitchen to make sure it was still safely tucked into her dresser drawer in her bedroom.

It looks like I'll have to use this for my junk so I won't have to eat, she thought. *Then again, maybe I could buy some frozen entrees and some paper and plastic dinnerware. Yeah, that's what I'll do.* Her mind was racing, yet she was proud of herself. She had actually elected to keep a clear head through all of this. "I need all the control I can get", she mumbled aloud.

She looked at the clock. It said eight-fifteen, which left her exactly fifteen minutes to get ready and get out of there for work. She dashed to her bedroom, all the while feeling a strange and oppressive presence in her apartment.

THREE

Denni actually arrived at work ten minutes early. She'd guessed that all these goings-on were leaving her more wired than she'd been in a while. She wasn't sitting at her desk for long though, until a tall, short-haired brunette bounded through the door. Her looks were not at all spectacular.

"I need to speak to Sophia Narring", she declared firmly.

Oh no, Denni thought. *Sophie.* The look on the brunette's face was threatening. Denni suddenly had a sinking feeling in her stomach.

"She's very busy in a meeting right now", Denni said, her voice almost wavering.

The woman stood there towering over Denni's desk, glaring at her. "I bet she is", she said.

Denni knew who the woman was before she even asked, but decided to do it anyway, just to play dumb. "May I say who *was* here?"

"I'm Dan's *wife*", she said, "and you can just stop trying to cover for your friend Sophia because I know that's she is sleeping with my husband." The woman's voice remained even and calm, but that glowering look continued throughout. "Now if you'll just excuse me." Dan's wife brushed past her and started towards Dan's office.

Following her, Denni yelled, "Wait! You can't go in there! There is a very important meeting going on with clients!"

Dan's wife paused as she reached for the doorknob and looked back at Denni. "I guess the meeting is going to have to take a slight break." She then proceeded to turn the knob and open the door.

Denni crept up past her to try to see if she would need to call the police. Dan's wife opened her husband's office door, and stepped backwards, almost landing in Sophie's chair. As soon as she opened the door, right in front of her, were Dan and Sophie. Apparently they did not hear the commotion outside of his office. She caught them right in the middle of the act, Sophie and Dan lying on top of his desk. All they could do was lay there and stare at her, shocked looks upon their faces.

Denni turned her face away and bit down hard on her arm to stifle a laugh. If she would have known what they were doing, she would have called Dan's office and at least told them to lock the door.

But how could she have known? They just got to work not even a half hour ago, for Pete's sake! If only Joy could see them now- man, would she have some things to say!

Where was Joy, anyway? Looking into the other part of the offices where Joy sat, she didn't see any evidence that she came in today. The only person she saw was her neighbor- Elizabeth "Liz" Pearson, the other "bible-thumper" in the office. Liz was different though- she was genuine, and didn't try to shove that stuff down people's throats. As a result, everyone did not run the other way when they saw her coming. Denni gave her a quick wave and a smile, which Liz returned.

Oh well, Denni thought, *it's just as good- Joy doesn't need to see or hear any of this, anyway. It would just give her more ammunition on why all kinds of things were going wrong with their lives and why they were all going to hell.*

"Tiffany, what in the *world* are you doing here?" Dan's voice bellowed from his office. Tiffany was regaining her composure and started advancing on Dan as he was zipping up his dress slacks. Probably Ralph Lauren pants, Denni guessed, or something like that. Sophie jumped up from the desk and smoothed her skirt down, barely looking at Mrs. Zimmerman. She knew the woman really wanted to kill her right about now, and wished nothing more than to disappear down into the floor. The entire two years she had been carrying on with Dan, she always knew that something like this was a possibility. She still was not prepared for it, however, now that it was happening right in front of her face.

Dan's wife was standing directly in front of him now, her eyes barely more than slits. "I'm here to put an end to your little affair, since you don't have the guts to. But it looks like you had to get one more in, huh?"

"What are you talking about?" Dan asked her in a casual tone. He knew that would just make her even angrier.

"What am I *talking* about? What just happened? I know it has been going on for quite some time. Besides, what did you expect since you told me about it and even *asked* me to end it for you? Let's see... what were your exact words? 'I'm tired of that clinging girl who acts like a child. She's spending too much of my money, even if the sex is better than it's been with you in a while.' That hurt, Dan, that really hurt.

But you know what? I can't blame her, Dan, I can only blame you. I bet she's wondered why, after all of this time, that you've never entertained the thought of leaving me. Have you *ever* talked about leaving me?"

Turning now to look at Sophie, she asked, "Has he ever told you he was definitely going to leave me?"

Sophie shook her head no. By now, tears were quickly and quietly streaming down her pretty face. She knew that Dan would never leave his wife, so they didn't ever bring the subject up. It was cheaper to keep her, as the saying went. But to hear the words come out of her mouth about the things Dan said... whether they were true or not, it hurt.

Tiffany was still looking at Sophie. In a softer tone, she said, "He's using you, honey. He's *been* using you. He comes home sometimes and tells me what you two did together. It's a challenge for me to try to beat your performance that day. Sometimes he waits until the morning and tells me so we'll do it then. I bet you smell my perfume on his skin those days, don't you?"

Sophie, tears still streaming down her face, turned to Dan. "Are you j-j-j-ju-just u-using me, Dan? *Are you*?" She was really crying now, and it was hard for her to get the words out. "I...I th-th-thought you c-c-ca-car-cared f-f-f-for m-m-me."

Dan just looked at her, spellbound. He never thought it would all end like this. He was used to getting exactly what he wanted, when he wanted it, and keeping it that way. His career, the house, the cars, his wife, his girlfriend... He never said all of those things to Tiffany. Sure, he told Tiffany about him and Sophie, but he just wanted to be honest- to get everything out in the open. He just wasn't in love with Tiffany anymore. He only told her about some times that Sophie and him were together to try to edge her away from him. It seemed to be having the opposite effect, though. He didn't want his affair with Sophie to end- he actually cared about her. Sure, it cost him a lot, but he had the money and he *wanted* to spend it on her. It was his choice. The only thing Sophie ever asked for was to spend time with him. And now it was going to be ruined if he couldn't convince her that everything Tiffany said wasn't true.

"Sophie, honey, I never told Tiffany I didn't want to be with you anymore." He put his hands on her arms and rubbed them.

Sophie just looked at him. Denni sighed to herself, careful that she wasn't heard. Was Sophie actually going to believe that pig?

Dan then turned to Tiffany. His voice still calm and even, he said, "You and I will talk later. This is the last straw, Tiffany. We will talk, but I am giving you twenty-four hours to get out of MY house."

"Your house?" She snorted. "*Your* house?"

"That's right- MY house. You never put a dime towards it. I paid for everything, and am still paying for everything. What have you paid for? You don't even have a job, which is partly my fault. I paid for everything you have."

Tiffany continued to glare at him with pure hatred, her eyes still merely slits. She knew she had lost- she just had to try to fight for her husband one last time. "I'll see that you continue to pay for everything for me", she hissed. She turned around sharply to face the door, her yellow nylon suit making a slight 'swishing' sound. Denni guessed that suit was probably an Armani, or something like that. She hurried up and ran back to her desk and sat down, busying herself with pretending to type something very engrossing on the computer. She knew any minute the brunette witch would be by.

Sure enough, she came briskly walking by without even a glance Denni's way. When she was out of the office building completely and on the sidewalk below, Denni breathed an audible sigh of relief.

Suddenly, Sophie popped in. "I know you know what was going on", she said with a smirk on her face.

Denni smiled at her, a big, broad smile. "You know me too well, girl", she said.

"He really cares about me, Denni, he really cares." Sophie's eyes were welling up again. "He told her to leave, you know."

"I know", Denni said.

"Now, maybe he and I can have a life together. That's all I wanted- to share my life with him."

"That's good, Sophie." Denni was still a little in shock with this morning's events. She couldn't imagine what all was going through Sophie's mind right now. Everything happened so fast.

Looking into her eyes, she asked, "Are you happy, Sophie? I mean, *really* happy?"

Sophie blinked at her, like she didn't understand why she was being asked this question. "Yes, I am", she finally answered. "Why wouldn't I be?"

Dan suddenly appeared in front of Sophie and Denni. "Why don't you girls take the rest of the day off? I have some business to take care of, and we've had enough excitement around here for one day. I'll see you tomorrow."

"But, what about the calls?" Sophie objected.

Dan raised his hand. "I'll just have Tom's office take care of them. We don't have any appointments today, anyway."

Tom Maddingdon was the other lead lawyer in the firm as well as the second half of the partnership. In fact, the name of the firm was Zimmerman and Maddingdon.

Tom was a dowdy fifty-something; nowhere near as attractive as Dan, who was only about three years younger than him.

"OK." Sophie was satisfied with that answer.

"I'll call you later", Dan said softly into Sophie's ear. She smiled at him as he walked away.

"Well, Denni, I'll see you tomorrow", Sophie said in a sing-song voice.

"See ya", Denni replied dreamily. She was in another world right now- a world where all her stuff was missing. She was anxious to get home to her apartment and see if all of it had reappeared. Surely she was imagining it all.

FOUR

Denni sat at her kitchen table and sighed loudly. This was the only piece of furniture that she had left besides her bed and dresser. Nothing had magically reappeared. She wasn't dreaming, after all.

What was really strange to her was the fact that she had a sense of peace in spite of it all, like losing most of her possessions was lifting a burden she had been carrying all of this time.

Denni thought maybe she should call Jim. She needed to feel better right about now, but man did she have a raging headache, in addition to being very very hungry. She thought she'd lie down for a little while before she called him.

She walked towards her bedroom, and strained to see inside of it. A cloud that was so dark it was almost black was hovering throughout the entire room.

Fear stabbed at Denni's entire being as she felt her stomach drop and heart start to race. She didn't want to go any closer to that almost black cloud, but she could feel herself being drawn in, mesmerized by its presence.

"What the *world??*" She asked herself out loud as she was drawn closer down the hall, closer to it. That cloud could be anything, although the first thought that came to her mind was a fire. She didn't smell any smoke, though.

As she neared, she could see what looked like eyes punched out of the mist. They were huge, and a little bit lighter than the rest of it, like a medium-gray storm cloud.

Denni was so scared she actually felt like she was going through the DTs. Her entire body was shaking, but she could not take her eyes off of that dark, hovering, motionless cloud. She was suddenly overwhelmed by a heavy feeling- a feeling like something really bad was going to happen- but she edged ever closer to it nonetheless.

She didn't have to step that far, however. The thing (whatever it was) now seemed to be coming towards her; *reaching* for her.

Denni had never been so scared in her entire life. Her heart was beating like she had just snorted some coke, except in a bigger quantity than she had ever done before. She wanted nothing else than to turn around and run, but she couldn't do either. Her body was frozen right where she stood.

All of a sudden, she felt something dripping from her nose. *This entire room has turned into a rainforest from this cloud*, she thought. When she was finally able to reach her hand up to her face to wipe the mist off, it came back full of blood.

Denni let out a scream that came from the bottom of her stomach, terror and panic written all over her face. She had to get out of there, and quick. She started to turn away so she could run, and was roughly jerked back.

The last thing she saw was the cloud entirely enveloping her as she felt an inward squeezing pressure and more blood dripping from her face.

\# \# \# \# \# \# \# \# \#

Jim was banging frantically on Denni's apartment door. She was supposed to call him over three hours ago, and she always called when she said she would. He had gotten worried when he finally called her five times and there still was no answer. Even more upsetting was the answering machine was not on. *Who knows what she could have gotten into*? He thought.

After the third try, he was able to bust her door open. "Third time's the charm", he muttered. She must not have had the deadbolt on.

The apartment was deathly quiet. Too quiet, in fact. He walked back towards Denni's bedroom, calling her name. He didn't want to take her by surprise, in case she had fallen asleep.

He stopped in mid-stride at her door, a look of horror on his face. Over the top of Denni's bed in big, block letters were these words: GOOD BYE, JIM. I LOVE YOU. They were written in blood.

\# \# \# \# \# \# \# \#

Over the next few days, Denni's neighbors were still talking about all of the screams they heard from apartment 2B, and about the man that ran from it and never stopped.

END

Entry Two- Deal with the Devil

ONE

8/14/06

LORD,

 IF ONLY I COULD UNDO THE DAMAGE I'VE DONE. BUT IT'S MUCH
TOO LATE. MY SOUL IS ETERNALLY DAMNED, AND IT'S GOING TO BE
COLLECTED ANY TIME TONIGHT...

 Note found at 815 Harwood Lane, Baltimore, MD

 Kathy Perkinson read the note left behind over and over again. It was brief, but it chilled her to the bone. This was not your run-of-the-mill missing persons case or homicide they were dealing with here.

 Even with her being on the Baltimore police force payroll for fifteen years now, she had never had any dealings with the occult. She would have preferred to keep it that way. Once those doors were opened, they were not easily closed.

 Kathy and her partner, Terry Amondis, were called to 815 Harwood Lane this evening on a report of strange noises coming from the row home. A little bit of investigating told them that this house was owned by a 23 year old white male named Richard Williams. His occupation was as normal as his name- he was a local truck driver.

 But that's where the humdrum activity stopped. After the two pulled up to the house and determined no one was home, they knocked on one of the neighbor's doors. They must have gotten the neighbor that called, because it was answered right away, with no hesitant looking-out-the-window-let-me-see-who-it-is-first.

 The sixtyish woman that was at the door stated that yes, she had seen Richard come in, but she did not see him come back out. She was always looking out of her windows and doors too, she told them emphatically. In the meantime, she heard guttural moans, groans, growling and some heavy thumps. He did not have any visitors come calling unless they arrived on foot.

After speaking to the woman and thanking her for her time, they decided to kick the door down. When they did and looked through the entire house, they confirmed for sure that the occupant was not home. That's when they had to start going through the house with a fine-toothed comb. Search warrant or not, they had to look through the house- from the neighbor's description, this occupant could be in a lot of danger and the first 48 hours were critical.

Kathy and Terry really did not discover anything out of the ordinary until they searched the basement. That was usually always the last place they looked. Believe it or not, anything they were going to find in different cases they worked was always on the first two floors; usually in the master bedroom.

So, after not finding anything besides the occupant's identity, they headed for the cellar.

That's where they hit pay dirt. The cellar itself was ordinary-looking; it had plain, cinder-block walls, and plenty of storage boxes along one side. Towards the back, they found a sanitary, or utility tub, sump pump, storage shelves, and a washer and dryer. They decided to look back in the front again, when they saw a small room off to the right side. As soon as they opened the door Terry stated, "I think our friend here is involved in the occult. I thought this stuff went out with the dark ages."

Kathy retorted, "*Was* involved."

Looking around, Terry felt she was right. This guy wasn't coming back anytime soon. Call it a cop's instinct. Amidst all of the black candles, makeshift altar, the note (which Kathy gripped tightly), journals, potions and ancient symbols, there was a long black streak of ash on one of the red walls. They also discovered some long, deep scratches on the wooden door to the room.

From the *inside*.

TWO

Richard Williams had been involved in the occult since the age of fifteen. At first, it started innocently enough and included some typical "dabbling": playing with the OUIJA board here, reading Tarot cards there. Basically, he was just curious. He would read spell books and books on the occult well into the night to broaden his knowledge and answer his questions but that was all. He and his circle of friends would play around and hold séances sometimes around two or three o'clock in the morning- the real witching hour. The séances showed minimal results for them- a little wind blowing around the house, chairs shaking- and that was about the extent of it. The occult was popular in its own right, but it seemed to him that the fervor and mystique were not as present as it was back in medieval times, and even as recently as the 1700s. Still, it and its powers were there, lurking in the background. Perhaps it was resting, waiting for when the time was right.

Occasionally, when there was something that he wanted, he would cast a spell or two to get the desired results. Most of the time it worked. He figured it couldn't hurt to get some "higher powers" to help with what he wanted. It was just practicing a little "white magic". Or so he thought. One day, a friend of his told him, "There *is* no such thing as 'white magic.' It's all involving dark powers. That's just a lie that Satan wants you to believe- that it's "good magic." You're selling your soul to get what you want either way. Any time you don't rely on God or Jesus Christ to provide for what you need, you're selling your soul!"

She went on further to explain to him that even though the "mystery and fervor" was not as much as it used to be, it was hidden in the background- tarot cards, OUIJA boards, affirmations and chanting, etc. It was Satan's way to disguise himself in these seemingly ordinary things to get people to do his bidding and take their focus away from God, as they may otherwise shy away from it if they knew they were really practicing the dark arts.

Elizabeth, or Liz as she liked to be called, was a Christian- of course she'd be against it. They had known each other since third grade. She had been trying to convert him ever since. Liz had not been a Christian the entire time, but she always believed that Jesus was the only way. When she would talk to Richard, he would just stare in her direction, a blank, far-away expression covering his face. Nothing that she said ever sank in. He just didn't want to hear it.

Now, Liz was afraid that something was wrong- *really* wrong. Lately, she had started to have premonitions and "feelings" about things, and they were always right. She felt that was more of her being anointed by the Holy Spirit.

Despite their differences, Richard and she had still managed to keep in touch at least once a month, with Liz gently reminding him to change his ways before it was too late. She just knew that no matter how many times she pestered him about becoming a Christian, they would still remain friends. As Liz was jiggling the door knob and peering into the windows for any signs of life, she was afraid that the reminders were no longer needed.

THREE

Terry jumped out of bed with a start, his heart pumping a thousand beats a minute. "That was *too* real", he mumbled to himself as he wiped the sweat off his forehead.

He padded down the stairs for a snack and to turn on the TV. He hardly ever had nightmares. The last one was the night before he was scheduled to testify in a huge murder case. That was five years ago. He didn't ever remember having any dream as real as this one, though.

He sat down in his recliner in front of the TV and propped his feet up. He was kind of chilly, so he reached for a blanket draped on one of the arms of the chair to cover himself up with.

Kathy and he did not find any signs of that Richard Williams guy today. There wasn't any reason to believe that he was dead, but then again, they also didn't have any proof that he was alive. They were going to have to go back to his house tomorrow and look for more clues. It was about time to get forensics in the picture, especially with that ash on the wall.

He was going to be dead tired later in the day. It was only two-thirty a.m. and he had three more hours until he *had* to get up, but he knew he'd never get back to sleep- nor did he want to.

He drew the blanket tighter around him. Yeah, they'd have to go back to that house tomorrow. He was not looking forward to it at all and nothing usually bothered him. The thought made him shiver uncontrollably.

That, and the vision of Richard Williams from his nightmare, running from an unseen terror, screaming "Help me, Kathy! Help me, Terry!!"

^ ^ ^ ^ ^ ^ ^ ^ ^ ^ ^ ^ ^

Liz slowly turned the front door knob to her friend Richard's house. It was unlocked. Surely he wasn't at home. She had only knocked about twenty times. Now she was worried.

^ ^ ^ ^ ^ ^ ^ ^ ^ ^ ^ ^

Terry and Kathy pushed the front door open and boldly walked inside. They figured there wouldn't be anyone in the house, so there was no need to be cautious.

^ ^ ^ ^ ^ ^ ^ ^ ^ ^ ^

Liz was staring up at the ceiling, a startled look crossing her face. She knew she had heard footsteps above her- she just *knew* it. She was walking around the perimeter of the basement, crouching down and looking for clues on the carpeted floor when she heard the ceiling creak above her. It was the floor boards in the living room. Now she stayed close to the floor, listening.

"Let's check the basement again", she heard a male voice say.

Now she was really in trouble. What if it was the police? They'd get her for breaking and entering and trespassing for sure. She got up and crouched down, making herself as small as she could, in the farthest corner of the back room, next to the washer. From there, a small door off to the side of the front room caught her eye. She'd just have to investigate that later. She had never been in this part of Richard's house before, so she had no clue as to what all was down here. For some reason, he never showed her the basement when he gave her a tour of his house. "It's just full of boxes from moving", he'd always say.

But she was in the basement now. She was always drawn to it- to come down here. It looked pretty neat to her- not messy at all. *Where did all those boxes go, Richard?* She thought sarcastically to herself.

The voices were coming down the stairs now. It sounded like it was more than two people; maybe one or two women and a couple of men.

"Yeah, he hasn't been to the meetings at all this week, and hasn't been answering the phone", one woman said. "I know it's just not like Richard, so that's why I called you guys- to come over with me."

"Well, we'll see what's going on", a gruff male voice said. "I think anything we're going to find out, we're going to find it here."

Liz pushed herself further up against the wall. She tried to make herself as invisible as possible. She barely even took a breath for fear of being discovered. She wanted to get a look at these people so bad, even though she had a feeling who they were. She had to go to the bathroom, too. That's OK- she just wasn't going to think about it. She could wait.

"Well, I don't see anything… hey, wait just a minute!" An excited male voice said. "What is this??"

Liz was dying to know, that's for sure.

"It feels kind of gritty in my fingers", the same voice said.

What was it?? Liz was just going to have to wait until they left. She was sure that whatever it was would still be there. She didn't really think they would need to take anything with them when they left. At least she hoped they didn't.

"Look at this!" A woman exclaimed. "Can you believe this? I never thought this stuff *really* happened."

"Do you think…" another woman said. Everyone was trying to talk at once.

"I don't know…"

"I guess that must be what happened…"

"I don't know if I want to be involved anymore…"

"I wonder what he was *into??*"

"What did he *do??*" The excitement level was very high.

"Let's get out of here", the gruff male voice said.

"Why are you in such a hurry?" A woman asked abruptly. "Is there something you know that we don't?"

"No, I don't know anymore about what happened here than you all do", he answered, "but this does not look good to me. In fact, it's getting to be a little scary. This brings into reality what we're playing around with here."

Liz furrowed her brows at this statement. *Playing around??* Is that what they really thought they were doing? They honestly acted as if they didn't even realize they were dealing with the devil himself. Playing around. Play time was never in the devil's, nor his slaves, vocabulary.

Liz could see that there were plenty of souls to be won, but she didn't think that it was a good idea to jump out and start preaching right now. As much as she wanted to, she was not prepared to die just yet. Or worse. They could decide to take her back with them.

FOUR

Terry and Kathy both let out a collective sigh. It had been about ten minutes since the group of people that broke into the back door of Richard Williams' place had left.

Both of them were caught by surprise, and had to take off running towards the coat closet in the living room. They were just on their way down to the basement when they heard the knob to the back door rattling furiously.

Whoever was there was going to get in one way or another for sure.

Terry and Kathy remembered that there was enough room in the coat closet for the both of them. They could have easily stayed and questioned whoever came in (and even open the door for them!) but they figured they might learn more just by hanging back, listening, and trying to see what they could. Besides, neither one of them wanted a confrontation just yet.

Dealing with drug dealers, pimps and even murderers was one thing. Dealing with satan worshippers was quite another, and it was one area with which they had no experience at all. This was the first time they had a case like this.

Terry turned to Kathy. "Are you ready to check the basement out now?" He asked. "Yeah, I think so. I hope those people didn't take anything on their way out."

Neither one had gotten a glimpse of any of them, let alone whatever (or whomever) they might be carrying out. That was the only bad thing about lying in wait until they were all gone- there was a chance that the evidence would no longer be around.

Slowly and quietly, they descended the stairs. When they reached the bottom, they stopped short. The door to the small room was ajar. Quickly, they drew out their guns at the same time. After twelve years of working together as partners, they almost thought exactly alike.

Liz thought she felt and heard something creeping up behind her, so she whirled around. There, facing her with guns drawn, was a man and woman. She threw her hands up in the air.

"I'm sorry! I didn't take anything! I only came in here to see what was going on with Richard. Honest!" She blurted.

Richard. So she personally knew this man who was getting more mysterious by the minute. Maybe she could shed much more light on the subject and perhaps help them close this case.

Terry and Kathy looked at each other. They were both thinking the exact same thing again.

^ ^ ^ ^ ^ ^ ^ ^ ^ ^

Night time was starting to creep upon the horizon. Daniel gazed up at the sky and the approaching pregnant moon. Pretty soon the time would be right to start the ritual. A séance this was not. He chuckled. Leave it to Richard to disappear around the time of a full moon.

He felt arms encircle his waist.

"Almost time, isn't it?" A warm female voice breathed into his ear.

"Yes, almost Ciara." He turned around and started kissing her with a feverish passion, then broke away. "We'll finish this later tonight. I only want to build up my energy for this."

"That's what I'm here for", she whispered as she unbuttoned her blouse, her diamond wedding ring glimmering from the moonlight pouring in the bedroom window. "I'm going to get you so excited that you can't help but have plenty of energy for tonight."

∧ ∧ ∧ ∧ ∧ ∧ ∧ ∧

"Well, Liz, you might as well start from the beginning", Kathy said to her. They were sitting on the brown leather sofa up in Richard's living room. None of them had wanted to stay in the basement right now. They really didn't care to stay in the entire house, but thought it best in case they needed to look for (or came upon) more clues.

"Well", Liz sighed, "Richard and I have known each other for about fifteen years now..."

"That's quite a while", Terry interjected. "How long has he had this ummm... problem?"

"Interested in the occult, you mean", Liz corrected.

"Well, I guess I should take that back and tell you that it was more than just interest. He was scalp-deep in that mess."

Terry and Kathy leaned forward a little more. They weren't going to hear her any better than they were hearing her now, but they didn't want to miss anything just the same. Also, it was never too late to learn something new.

Liz continued. "If you couldn't tell by looking around downstairs, he was into black magic. I say black magic because of the fact that he performed rituals, spells, and conjured demons, which did his bidding. Rituals to conjure the demons, and demons to carry out his spells. " Liz stopped talking. She could hear herself saying much more than she needed to.

"Demons, huh?" Kathy wanted to laugh out loud but didn't. Demons. It sounded like something that came out of a fairy tale. A fairy tale that Liz seemed to know a lot about.

She started scribbling in her little notepad that she carried around with her all the time and decided to entertain her. "Did any of this 'stuff' actually work?" She felt that it was a really dumb question especially since she didn't believe in anything, but one that needed to be asked regardless.

"I suppose. He hardly ever talked about that stuff with me. He knew I was totally against it, being a Christian."

Kathy's ears perked up as she took more notes in her little book again. Just what was this "Christian" stuff about anyway? It sounded to her like another fairy tale.

"So what did you two normally talk about?" Terry asked.

"Well, like I said, we've known... I mean *had* known each other about fifteen years, so it wasn't like we became friends yesterday. He wasn't always like this, and neither was I. He had gotten into this around age fifteen, and I didn't really become a Christian until about a year ago, so we almost had mutual interests. *Almost.*"

∧∧∧∧∧∧∧∧

Evan started to turn away from the upstairs bedroom at Daniel's house when he heard Daniel's voice yell out at him.

"It's OK, Evan, come in", he called. The door had been closed.

"I wasn't sure if you were even in there", Evan said as he walked in. Ciara had already finished getting dressed about ten minutes ago. Her and Daniel had fooled around a little to the point where both of them were extremely excited, almost like their honeymoon night. The energy level was still very high, and Daniel's eyes had a very wild and bright look about them.

"Well, I guess you need a little more time", Evan said. "When do you plan on going to the site?"

"We'll leave in about fifteen minutes", Daniel replied. "I want to finish preparing."

"I'll tell the others", Evan said as he walked out and shut the door.

The "site" was a spot deep in the woods about thirty minutes from Richard's house. There was a very old graveyard there as well. They knew that Richard would have wanted to be buried there, if there was any part of him at all to be interred. Richard was gone and was never coming back. Daniel just knew it. Those woods were where Richard did most of his rituals. He had never wanted to kill an animal or a person and have its blood in his house. Everyone had warned him against it; especially the main four:

Evan, Daniel, Ciara and Bethany. It was a known rule to never kill any living thing for a ritual. The energy in the killing and dying would almost always be used against the conjurer.

Evan shook his blonde head sadly. *Everything happens for a reason,* he thought. If for nothing else, at least it verified the fact that there was indeed a hell, and that their efforts weren't wasted.

He signaled to the others that it was almost time. Everyone would be silent from now until the point when they reached the site. They were all sitting around on the main floor of the house, patiently waiting to go. Everyone wanted to get their minds and energy prepared for the ritual.

Daniel came down the stairs and started out the front door, the others following behind him.

∧∧∧∧∧∧∧

Kathy, Liz and Terry were sitting at a medium-sized wooden table in one of the interrogation rooms at the Baltimore police station, Liz on one side, Kathy on the other, and Terry standing off to the left of her.

"Tell me more about what you and Richard did together and talked about", Terry said to Liz.

"Well, there isn't very much more to tell, just regular young adult stuff. Before I was saved, we went to the bars and clubs pretty regular. I was never much of a drinker, but I held my own a night or two. We hung out at least twice a month, and always tried to keep in touch by phone once a week. We've constantly remained close, except in that one part of his life that he refuses, um… to talk to me about. He would never want to discuss it with me unless I would be on his side." Liz just wasn't sure if she should talk about him in the past tense or not. It was all so surreal.

"Were you two ever involved?" Kathy asked.

Liz had to smile a little on this one. Now just why would a cop want to know about that? Or even care? Maybe they thought that there was a crime committed. A crime of passion. "No, never; I just don't think we were ever really attracted to each other. Probably because we had known each other for so long and had been through a lot together. I know I thought of him as a brother, so I'm sure he felt the same way about me." Liz smiled again slightly. They (or she, she wasn't sure which yet) had so many good memories, even the ones where they just fooled around slightly- a kiss on the lips here, a hug there.

Kathy noticed the far-away look in her eyes. Even though she felt that there was a little more to Richard and Liz's relationship than what Liz was telling them, and possibly more to Liz's story itself, she thought this time that there was really no need to investigate further- it seemed to be an open-and-shut case on the occult. At least as far as it concerned Liz, anyway.

"You and him really had some good times together, didn't you?" She asked her.

"Yes, even after our differences became more and more evident", Liz replied. "I'm sorry I really can't help you more with all of this- I'm just trying to figure out what happened to Richard myself."

"Do you know if he had any enemies?" Terry asked, taking a couple of steps closer to the table.

"No, not that I know of", Liz replied. "I can't even tell you who his friends were either, since he hid such a big part of his life."

"You don't know any friends or acquaintances at all?" Terry's eyes narrowed. "What about his family? We're going to need to get in touch with them."

"We had some mutual friends that I've lost touch with since, but I can provide their info that I had last", she said.

"As far as his parents and sister, I have their current numbers and addresses. In fact, I called them this morning to see if he had contacted them or if they knew where he was at and they had not heard from him either- they were getting ready to file a missing person report."

"We'll be visiting them as well", Kathy said. "Just to see if they know anything at all that's different than what we have found out." Which of course, wasn't much. About all they knew at this time was Richard was into devil worshipping and that he had disappeared. They had no signs of foul play, unless they counted the ash and scratches that they found, nor did they have any reason to believe that there was. They were pretty sure Liz felt the same way.

Kathy gave Liz a pad of paper and a pen so she could start writing down names, addresses and phone numbers of Richard's contacts. Everywhere they had searched in his home, they did not find an address book, or anything else like that written down. They did not see a computer in the home, either, nor did they find a cell phone yet. They figured he had to have had a really good memory, or everyone just contacted him instead.

"I have to come back or call with the rest of the addresses and phone numbers; I only remember his parents' and sister's info", Liz said.

"That's OK; just give us a call with it- please try to do so within the next day. We really need to try to find Richard and wrap this case up", Kathy said, even though deep down she felt that finding him was out of the question. "Do you have any other questions, Terry?" She looked behind her to her partner.

"No, not at this time. Just don't go leaving the state any time soon, Liz." He was staring at her as if she was a criminal. He just had a hard time believing that Richard did not have any enemies at all with what he was involved in. He also had a hard time believing that Liz did not know any more about who he hung out with than she did. It was possible, but he still didn't believe it. Not one bit.

"I don't have any plans to do so", Liz said dryly, getting up from her chair. She really did not like cops or trust them, either. Kathy was OK, but Terry fit her standard idea of them- always judging people, always ready to accuse someone of wrongdoing. She did not like when people judged others- she didn't like to feel that way, but she thought that they were going to have a lot to answer for in front of the Lord.

Kathy, sensing Liz's sudden change of mood, got up and extended her hand. "That is all for now", she said.

Liz shook Kathy's hand. "Have a good day", she replied, addressing both of them. She walked out.

FIVE

Liz smiled as she opened the door to her four-bedroom townhome. She was very relieved to be home after spending almost two hours at the downtown police station. She hoped that she wouldn't have to go back anymore. She was sure that nothing else could be done.

Nothing else, that is, until Liz looked up from dropping her keys on the floor and saw the shadowy figure standing before her.

A stab of fear gripped her heart and stomach, as she gripped her keys tightly in her fist. Without the figure saying a word, Liz felt that it- Richard- was telling her to go back to his house, which she was planning to do, anyway.

Still tightly clutching her keys, she spun around to go back out of the front door.

^ ^ ^ ^ ^ ^ ^ ^ ^ ^ ^ ^ ^

Walking up to Richard's front porch- or what *used* to be Richard's front porch, anyway- Liz was wondering how in the world she was going to get in. And if she did get in, she really hoped the police would not make another appearance for the evening.

Peering in the sidelight that was next to the front door, all appeared to be quiet and dark. So far, so good. Liz tried the door handle- it was locked up tight. She decided to walk around to the back door, thinking that maybe someone from the forensics team forgot to lock it. She was right, and quickly locked it behind her after she got in.

She was finding herself drawn to the basement again. Here she had never been able to go down there at all while he was alive, and now she was going to be seeing it twice in less than two days.

She flipped on the light and bounced down the stairs as quickly as possible. She just wanted to get in this basement, do what she had to do, and get out, because she did not know if anyone else would have the same idea.

Walking across the front of the basement, she stopped at the wooden door to that small mysterious room. It was ajar, so she pushed it open, walked in, and flipped on the light. She scanned the shelves on the walls and the various books that were on them- books on rituals, spells and the like. One of the books looked very old. Grabbing it, she shoved as much of it in her purse as she could. She would take a look it when she had time. Maybe it would give her more insight on what actually happened to Richard. Among the other books were a couple of full-sized skull replicas (or were they?) with and without devil horns, different color candles (mostly black) and candle holders. Walking over to the small counter-height table in the middle of the room, her eyes then stopped at something down on the shiny brown painted concrete floor in the right corner.

Liz stepped over to that corner, squatted down, and took a closer look. It was a sizable pile of ash.

"Hmmm... I wonder what this is? I guess maybe he was burning things down here for his rituals?" Liz said out loud to herself. "I wonder why the cops didn't find this and take it?"

Maybe they thought that's what it was too- or maybe they already took a sample. She then ran her right hand through it and stopped short, landing backwards on her rear end, eyes widened in surprise.

This was no normal ash. It was very gritty to the touch, and when Liz had ran her hand through it, she felt something hard and sharp.

She got on her knees and leaned towards the pile. Reaching for it, she sifted the gritty ash in her right hand again.

When she finally saw the sharp pieces, she let out a loud gasp. She was no medical examiner, but she instantly knew what it was nevertheless. It was bone fragments. "Oh...my...Lord..." she breathed. At that instant, it became apparent to her where Richard had went. He was right here, in this corner. There was only one way it could have happened, too, and no one would ever believe it but her...

Just then, she felt someone behind her. Whirling around, she saw a dark, smoky, semi-transparent figure. It had red glowing eyes.

Remaining calm, she said loudly, "What is it that you want? If you think you can take me with you too, you'd better guess again."

The figure advanced towards her, making her eyes widen in horror. Her left hand flew up to her mouth to cover a scream. She realized it was Richard, back from the dead and from the bowels of hell. How he was ever able to do that, Liz did not know.

He came a little closer. "Help me, Liz!!" He screamed. His voice was thunderous and gravelly. "Help me get out of here!!"

Liz wondered how he could possibly be talking and standing in front of her right now. Unless it really wasn't Richard.

Liz always believed that once people went to Heaven or hell, and they had to go one place or the other, they did not come back. Sure, she believed that maybe once in a while God may allow someone to come back and help a loved one, or come to help take them home to Heaven, but if someone went to hell, well, they weren't coming back. As for ghosts, she believed that it was demons impersonating people so that they could remain hidden- their true form wouldn't be seen and scare people away. Or, it really was ghosts of people- people being kept on earth by demons for their purposes. It was all part of their plan...

In this case, however, she believed that it really was Richard. How he was able to be here talking to her right now, though, she was anxious to find out.

"Richard, I can't do anything for you- it's too late! I warned you plenty of times before! Why didn't you ever listen?" Her eyes were filling with tears. "Didn't you ever believe that it was all true? Satan is the only one that lies and deceives- he tells and shows you whatever you want until he gets what *he* wants- and it's always what *he* wants in the end- your soul!!"

Richard started to cry; a painful look coming over his face. "It is so horrible here, Liz", he said. "The air is so dense and hot you can't breathe. My whole body is in pain. I am being tortured every second. The very demons I conjured are the ones that came to get me. Everyone moaning, screaming and crying for God to help them all the time. But God never answers."

Liz just stood there with tears in her eyes, listening to him tell her about the nightmare she knew in her heart to be true.

"This is nothing like I thought it would be, Liz", he said. "I thought I would have an honored position…"

And at that moment, slash marks started appearing on his body. There was no need for Liz to ask him how he was able to be standing there in front of her.

Liz heard nothing but his tortured screams as the figure of Richard burst into flames and then disappeared as quickly as it came.

^ ^ ^ ^ ^ ^ ^ ^ ^ ^ ^ ^

Liz was still breathing pretty heavily, a light film of perspiration on her brow and back. "He was standing right there", she said, pointing to the spot in the little room. "He was standing right at the door."

Terry and Kathy had both gotten the feeling that Liz was going to try and go back to Richard's place, so they had decided to follow her. Call it detective's instinct, they told her. Motioning over to the ash, she said, "I didn't touch anything else other than part of that. It seems like that's where Richard disappeared, alright…"

Terry was already on the phone. "Get me forensics, right away." They had already been here, how in the world did they ever miss that? Unless… unless they didn't want to go in that little red room at all.

Forensics would be over to the house in about an hour, or less, which if Terry wanted to be honest, he didn't know if he could hang around that long. He was starting to feel a little sick.

Waves of slight dizziness and nausea were starting to wash over him as well as a feeling of "heaviness." He normally never felt this way- always very meticulous about staying out of public bathrooms as much as possible, rarely ate out in restaurants or fast-food joints, and kept his hands so clean that they were chapped and dry. He just did not have time to be sick, even if only for a couple of hours, so he tried to do what he could to keep himself well.

Deep down, he had an idea of what was bringing this feeling of discomfort on, but he had to test his theory out. "Excuse me for a moment", he said to Kathy and Liz. "I need to get some air."

Liz had seen the look that was on Terry's face once before and gazed at him knowingly. "You'll be alright. Just stay outside for a couple of minutes."

Terry nodded, and walked back upstairs to go out the front door. The exterior basement door was blocked and unusable. He decided to wait on the front step for forensics, taking in huge gulps of chilly December air.

"You know, there's a cure for that", Liz said as she came out on the front porch. "You may want to try Him sometime", she added as she placed a tract in Terry's hand. This time, Terry took it and placed it in his pocket. He really would read it this time.

After Liz had finished telling Kathy everything that happened, she was told to go on ahead home. There was nothing else here that she could do, and she needed to go before forensics came. If they had any more questions, they would call or stop by. Liz was more than happy to oblige- this whole mess with Richard was making her exhausted.

Just then, Kathy appeared at the door. "Just thought I would check on you, Terry", she said as she came out on the front porch, handing him his coat.

"I'll be fine", he said. In fact, he was feeling one hundred percent better already. He still was going to wait until forensics came before he went back in that house though.

He looked up at Liz. "This stuff is real, isn't it?"

Liz was glad that it was finally starting to sink in with Terry. "Yes, I'm afraid it is", she said. "Good night."

"Good night, Liz", Kathy and Terry said in unison.

Liz got in her car and drove home, hoping that she would be able to get some sleep.

SIX

"Richard, come back to us!!" Daniel's voice thundered over the fire as he spoke the last of the ritual, his arms raised in the air. He as well as the rest of the group truly believed they could conjure Richard and be able to communicate with him.

"Show yourself to us again, from the depths of hell!!" Daniel yelled. They all believed that Richard had an honored position and would be available to do all of their bidding.

This ritual would seal the deal, although they all knew the risk and the price involved- at least one, if not all of their souls.

Daniel lowered his arms and continued to stare at the site where they all had held many, many rituals.

Just then, Daniel fell to the ground. The sound of a hundred voices laughing together filled the air. The earth started to swallow Daniel's legs; and then spit him back up ten feet in the air. He came back down with a thud that shook the trees that were surrounding everyone.

Evan, Ciara, Bethany and the others were all standing around dumbfounded with blank stares on their faces. They had a slight idea what was happening, but they wanted to deny it just the same.

Suddenly, the figure of Richard shot up out of the ground where Daniel was lying in a state of shock. Richard's body was a smoky color, and he had red glowing eyes. He must have stood about eight feet tall, or so it seemed. When he spoke, it was a voice of total authority, and one to be feared. This was not the Richard that they had known.

"What's the matter, Daniel? Why are you looking so surprised?" Richard taunted him. "Your rituals had always worked before, what makes you think they wouldn't work now?"

His voice sounded like it had many other voices speaking along with it in the background.

Daniel rose to his feet, a grimace of pain marking his face. He started to back away towards everyone. The figure of Richard raised its arms towards him, and Daniel was stopped right in his tracks.

"Just where do you think you're going, Daniel?" Richard's voice boomed. "You encouraged me and promised me all these great rewards I would have if I worshipped your devil." Richard sounded even angrier now. "Don't think you're going to leave without getting yours", he continued. "Or yours." He looked at one of the girls to his right and raised his arm in her direction. She was pulled back to the group, Richard having caught her trying to sneak away. "You know, I could show all of you a vision of what this is like, and it's just like the name says, hell, so you could know what you're up against…"

Everyone was staring at Richard, too afraid to even think about moving, because they all knew he could read their minds as well.

"But you know what?" He finally continued after a dramatic pause. "I'm gonna do one better than that!" He yelled.

At that moment, the last thing that was heard was the sound of thirty-five screams as everyone disappeared in a huge ball of flame.

^ ^ ^ ^ ^ ^ ^ ^ ^ ^

Clutching the red rose tightly in her hand, Liz was nearing the spot that Richard had shown her so long ago. It had been a while since she had been anywhere near his house or any place else having to do with him. If she was honest with herself, she was a little spooked from his last visit to her and she didn't want to do anything at all to encourage him further.

"That's really silly of me", she chided herself aloud. "I think he should know by now that there's no chance of him ever coming back."

The air was still for almost the end of January, but she pulled her coat closer around her anyway. She was feeling chilly all of a sudden.

Finally, she reached the clearing in the middle of the woods and stopped at a calf-high pile of ashes. She didn't have to think too long to know what it was.

Liz bent down a little and placed the rose on top of the pile. The realization of why she was strongly drawn here today made her shiver a little as she stared at the ashes.

She blinked a couple of times, hard, and suddenly stood up. Liz could have sworn she saw a face, Richard's face, imprinted in those ashes. Just then, the lips in the ashes moved. "Help me, Liz!!" They yelled. "Help me!!"

Just then, a big gust of wind blew as Liz started to run. The ashes were after her now, and they were gaining fast.

Liz ran as hard as she could, lungs straining to handle the huge doses of bitter cold air. She did not look back, even upon reaching her car. She drove home like a madwoman, avoiding red lights at all costs, praying she would not have an accident.

Upon reaching her house, she jammed the car in park, ripped out her keys and ran to her front door. Flinging it open, she decided to glance back and saw that the ashes were right behind her.

She slammed and locked the door, which had now begun to shake.

Liz sat up in her bed with a start, sweat rolling down her back and sunlight streaming through her window. She breathed a big sigh of relief and smiled. She loved to see her bedroom filled with sunlight, and was so grateful that it was daytime when she woke up and not the middle of the night.

She looked down at the floor, and just where the ray of sun shone on it was a small pile of black ashes.

A single black rose lay on top.

END

Entry Three- Warning

Prologue

"I'll be back- I really have to go", Lou Steton yelled to a few of his waiting team mates as he was running to the woods. They were almost finished playing their last softball game of the evening, but he couldn't wait any longer. He headed back to the middle of the woods where lots of trees and bushes were and he thought no one could see him if they tried. He unzipped his softball pants and looked around. There wasn't anyone else nearby, but it was a habit- you had to make sure no one was spying on you. He looked down at the bush in front of him as he zipped his pants back up. What a relief to be done.

Lou blinked fast a couple of times- he thought he saw something underneath of that bush.

His heart almost jumped out of his chest when all of a sudden, a horrible demonic face was staring back up at him from the ground in front of the bush.

"Hi, Lou", it said softly to him as it started to be more than just a face. Hands started to appear, and then arms, and it was then reaching, grabbing for him…

ONE

Alisa Monsfeld stood in her expansive gourmet kitchen that was in her 8,000 square-foot colonial, holding her breath. She could have sworn she heard footsteps upstairs.

She rolled her eyes upward towards the ceiling, for some reason thinking it would help her hear a little better. Her husband Jack was not due home for at least another twenty minutes, and when he did come home, the whole neighborhood knew- the man did not know what it was like to be quiet at all.

Alisa glanced over at the security alarm control pad and breathed a sigh of relief. The light on the panel still showed a steady red, meaning that the alarm was on and no windows or doors were open. Still, they did have an attic upstairs that even though it was unfinished, may still provide access to a determined criminal...

THUMP!! THUMP!! There it was again- she *knew* she was not imagining things this time.

Quickly and quietly, she slipped out of the kitchen and went towards the mud room, where the door that led to the garage was. She opened it, leaning against it to keep things as quiet as possible. Good thing she didn't have this door hooked up to the alarm- yet- or it would have been going off. She sure hoped Jack didn't move things around in there too much. Normally, he was very organized, but when he had something on his mind especially having to do with a car...

She flipped the overhead garage light on and scanned the room. There it was on the floor in front of the spare tire- the tire iron. It was an older one- made with American steel and very heavy.

She ran over to it, grabbed it as fast as she could, turned back around and ran out of the door, flipping the light back off and closing the door almost at the same time. She didn't bother to lock it back up in case she had to make that her exit.

Thump THUMP *THUMP*!!! There it was again, making her heart skip a couple of beats this time. Whoever it was, they were either going through every closet and drawer up there, or they were intentionally making that noise- to get her to come up.

She slipped back out to the kitchen and grabbed her cordless phone, getting ready to dial 911. Thumb paused over the buttons, she had second thoughts of dialing. What if it really was her imagination? The alarm was not going off; the display still showing every door and window closed tight.

But what if it wasn't her imagination?

Thinking the better of it, she dialed. Better to face the penalty of a false alarm then to have someone ransack her whole house with her in it, or worse.

The phone was picked up before the second ring was finished. "911, what's your emergency?" A female voice asked on the other end.

Crouching down on the floor behind her kitchen island, Alisa told her in a half-whisper to please send someone right away; she thought there was an intruder in her home.

When the voice on the other end asked Alisa to remain calm and to verify her location, she froze. She started to hear footsteps coming down the stairs LEADING DIRECTLY TO THE KITCHEN.

"Ma'am? Are you still there? Ma'am?" The voice started to get more insistent; the footsteps getting closer.

"I'm OK, my address is…" Alisa said in a whisper while falling to her knees and crawling as quickly as she could to the dining room. There were curtains in there that came all the way to the floor and then some- she could hide behind one of those.

Getting to the dining room, she finished giving the dispatcher her address and then hung up. She still had the tire iron tightly gripped in her other hand. Before diving behind one of the curtains, she cocked her head to one side, trying to listen for the footsteps between her heavy breathing and heartbeat. They had stopped, which was never a good sign.

Just when she was getting ready to pull one of the curtains over her, she heard the garage door open. *"Thank God!"* She breathed- Jack was home. She had to warn him of an intruder though, but could not move out of fear. She did not know where this person was in the house now.

She made herself as small as possible behind the curtain making sure everything was covered, and dialed his cell phone. *Please answer, please answer,* she kept repeating in her mind. Usually when Jack saw the house number on his cell when he was already home, he would just come inside to find out what she wanted.

She heard him close the door to his car and tinker with some of the tools on top of his toolboxes.

Answer the phone, she screamed in her head.

Just then, the curtain moved, revealing the tattered bottom of a black robe-like fabric. Alisa swallowed hard, every fiber of her being screaming to run, but she could not move.

As she was deciding whether to try to run or take a swing at whomever or *whatever* this was, the curtain was roughly yanked away. Standing in front of her was a tall, dark figure with even darker, soulless "pits" where the eyes should have been. Alisa could not stop staring into these pits, and as she was doing so, was overcome with the greatest fear and despair she had ever known. She had never felt such a mix of strong emotions before.

The fear decided to take over as Jack finally opened the interior garage door, stepping inside to the screams of Alisa.

* * * * * * * * * * * *

Elizabeth Pearson closed her King James Version bible, a thoughtful look on her face. She was preparing for her bible study group tonight. They were going to start analyzing her favorite chapter, Revelations. She just loved that chapter. There were so many ways to interpret what was written. It was very fascinating and scary too. Every time she read it, she was comforted by knowing that she wasn't going to be around when the prophecies came to pass.

She had about an hour until she had to get to church, so she decided to go ahead and fix herself a light supper. She had just gotten in from work thirty minutes ago.

The phone suddenly rang, interrupting her search in the fridge. "Hello?" She asked.

"Liz, is that you?" The voice on the other end sounded hurried and breathless.

A sharp stab of fear pierced her stomach. "Jack, is everything all right?" She was almost afraid to ask.

"Alisa's just been admitted to the hospital, can you meet us here?"

"Oh. My. Lord." Liz sank to the floor.

"Meet us up on the fifth floor of North General."

"Fifth floor?" Liz wasn't too familiar with that hospital, but at least she knew it wasn't the emergency room.

"Yeah, Liz, the fifth floor…the psychiatric ward."

* * * * * * * * * * * *

Louis Steton stood in front of the men's room mirror, washing his hands. He had decided to take a break for a little while after losing one thousand dollars at the slots. He was really hoping to win tonight, not lose. He really couldn't afford to lose at all anymore, but he just couldn't stop coming to the casino.

He splashed some water on his face. All of a sudden, the room was starting to get really hot.

Was it him, or was it starting to get dark too? He splashed some more water on his face and rubbed his eyes. The room *was* getting dim. He looked up at the ceiling- there were no lights that were out. He felt his pulse- it was normal. He wasn't having a heart attack, but he still wondered if he was going to black out.

He turned the water on full blast to let it get really cold. That's what he needed-some ice cold water. He was just upset from losing too much at the slots.

He bent down to sip some cold water through his hands and bolted upright. Someone was in the room with him. He thought for sure that he was alone, but he *felt* another presence in the room, the same feeling that you get when someone is standing behind you.

Bang! He kicked open the door to the first stall with his foot, causing it to hit the wall behind. No one was there. He moved to the other three. *Bang! Bang! Bang!* No one in sight, or at the urinals either.

He went back over to the sink. Now he was getting delusional. *Calm down, Lou,* he told himself. *You're going to walk out of this bathroom and out of the casino. No one is in here, and you don't owe anybody, so no one is stalking you.*

He looked into the mirror to smooth his hair before leaving. It was starting to turn black- just like if you were to put a ninety percent tint over it. All of a sudden, a reaper appeared behind him. His heart leaped up into his throat. It was just like those reapers that you see pictures of all over the place around Halloween. It had a tattered black robe with a hood draped low on its head. In one skeletal hand it held a long, sharp gleaming scythe. The other hand it held out to Lou, beckoning. Behind him was a wall of fire, and behind that, a slot machine.

* * * * * * * * * * * *

Liz walked as fast as she could through the front doors of the hospital, hoping she didn't knock anyone over as she passed them by. She didn't know why she was in such a hurry- it wasn't like Alisa was going anywhere soon. In fact, they probably had her so drugged up right about now, she probably couldn't even *think* about leaving, let alone make good on it. Nevertheless, she was still anxious to see her sister and let her know everything was going to be just fine.

She ran as fast as she could up each flight of stairs. There was no time to wait for the elevator. At least North General didn't have the psych ward in the basement like at some hospitals. First floor, second floor…finally, she burst through the door to the fifth floor.

"Alisa Monsfeld, please", Liz said breathlessly to the on-duty nurse.

"Room 510, just down the hall to your left", she said.

"Thanks." When Jack called, he didn't have a room number yet. All he knew was the floor they would be on.

Alisa peeked into room 510 before walking in. She was half expecting Alisa to be writhing around uncontrollably in a strait jacket, foam coming out of her mouth, and half expecting her to be lying in bed staring blankly at nothing, drool slowly creeping its way down towards her pillow.

She took a deep breath. No matter what state her sister was in, she was just going to have to face it. Alisa needed Liz, her baby sister, more than she ever had.

"Lord, please give me strength", Liz breathed.

"Hi Jack". Liz said, grabbing both of his hands and squeezing.

Jack steadily met her gaze. "She's heavily sedated. The nurse said she probably won't even start to come out of it for about two hours."

"Well, that leaves us enough time for you to tell me just what in the world is going on." Liz glanced over at Alisa, who was for now sleeping peacefully.

"I'll tell you everything I know, which isn't much. What I do know, enough, well…"

"Well, *what?*" Liz was normally a very patient girl, but this was her *sister* here, and she just had to know, right *now*.

"Liz, what I do know, well, it may be enough that they would try to keep her here."

Liz let out a harsh sigh. She knew that just might be one of the possibilities. She didn't believe in psychiatric medicine herself.

"Did the doctor say anything?" Liz's voice held a little hope.

"No, only the nurses saw her so far. I think they said the doctor will be around to see her tomorrow, so he can decide which way to go."

"Oh…why don't we go to the lounge or something and you can tell me what happened?" Liz started out of the room. Alisa did not know she was there anyway…yet.

They walked into the lounge on the fifth floor and sat down at one of the tables. Jack started out by telling Liz of the screaming wife he came home to…

* * * * * * * * * * *

Doug Troland strolled through the foyer of his eighteen-thousand square foot house, whistling. Another day where the profits went through the roof at the overseas trading company where he was the CEO. He smiled to himself. It would probably be another record-breaking year where his salary and perks would top thirty million dollars. He rubbed his hands together enthusiastically. Time to get another offshore bank account.

His six year old daughter Melanie ran to greet him. "Daddy!" She yelled excitedly.

"Hey honey, how was your day?" Doug gave his daughter a big bear hug.

"It was fine, Daddy, except I got another visit from the ugly man." A small frown crossed her face briefly.

Doug's smile faded. This was not the first time he heard of this "ugly man". Melanie had been talking about him appearing to her for several weeks now. He only came during the day when Melanie was home, usually after she came in from school. When asked what he looked like, Melanie said that he had a lot of lines across his face, like deep wrinkles, bright yellow eyes, pointed ears, and stood a lot taller than Doug, which would have had to have been at least six feet to beat his five-eleven. She also said that he had broken yellow teeth and very long, sharp fingernails. He also had a bad smell, "kind of like poop", she said.

Doug really didn't believe in demons which is what this "ugly man" sounded like, or hell for that matter, but he didn't have any reason to doubt his daughter either. An imaginary friend was one thing, but he was quite sure if Melanie was going to have one, it would not look like *that*.

"Well, honey, what did he say to you today?" The "ugly man" always appeared to Melanie and only her, said something and then disappeared.

"He said you better enjoy all that money that you're making, because this is your heaven right here on earth."

Doug took a step back, a shocked look on his face. There was no way Melanie could have made that up. They never discussed religious matters, including heaven.

"He said he's got you right where he wants you, and he's coming for you soon. He said that he's going to make sure he's right there to take you home with him. Where are you going, daddy?" Melanie had a curious look on her face as she stared up into his.

"Nowhere, honey. Daddy's not going anywhere. As scared as he was starting to feel, no one was going to come after him. He would build a fortress around this house if he had to.

"C'mon, honey, let me tuck you in." It was Melanie's bed time; eight-thirty. Doug made sure that if he couldn't get home any earlier, that he would definitely be home in time to see her off to bed. "You know what, honey?"

"What's that, daddy?" Melanie's long brown hair bounced as she trotted up the winding staircase.

"Let me talk to Mommy about it first, but I think we should go on a nice vacation soon. Anywhere you'd like to go." It would only be the family's fifth vacation so far that year. Doug's employees were real lucky if they could afford to take that many vacations in a lifetime.

"*Anywhere?*" Melanie had a mischievous look in her eyes.

"Anywhere, honey. You think about it and let me and Mom know sometime tomorrow, OK?"

"OK!" Melanie jumped up into the air and then ran into her spacious bathroom which was in her huge bedroom decorated in pink and purple to brush her teeth.

Doug sat down on the edge of her bed to wait until she was finished and grabbed a book. He usually read about five pages to her a night before it was lights out.

As he started flipping through the book to find where he left off (he was so distracted about his money last night he forgot to put the bookmark in) he caught a faint whiff of sewage.

"Hmmmm…" he said to himself while Melanie was brushing away. "I guess it's time to get a plumber in here to see what's going on with these pipes."

But deep down, Doug knew it wasn't the pipes. It wasn't the pipes at all.

That smell was a warning of what was to come.

* * * * * * * * * *

Liz took the last sip of her coffee and winced. She had been listening to Jack intently for the past half hour and her coffee was freezing. She hadn't wanted to stop and get a fresh cup, however.

Jack laid his hands down on the table. He was finished telling his story; what he knew, anyway. He looked away, his sandy-colored hair shining from the fluorescent lights. He wanted to give Liz a couple of minutes to take it all in.

Liz took a deep breath, her mind racing. She was always ready to hear tales of the supernatural, but never dreamed that one of them would take place in her own family, or even be happening again after the issues with Denni and then Richard last year. The whole feeling was so surreal.

Before she had a chance to say anything, however, a doctor appeared.

"Nurse Wilson said I might find you two here", the black-haired, deeply tanned man standing in front of them said. He pulled out a chair and sat down.

"Mrs. Monsfeld will probably be waking up within the next half hour or so, and then I would like to spend a little time speaking with her." When she had come in, her eyes as wide as pie plates with fear, he had not been able to coax one word out of her.

"That would be great", Jack said. "Do you have any idea what might be wrong with her?"

"I won't know until I spend some time observing her", the doctor said. Liz glanced over at his name tag. It said 'David Kendall, M.D.' That was a good doctor's name.

He looked at Jack. "I was hoping you could fill me in. Was she exhibiting any unusual behavior before she was brought in tonight?"

Jack shook his head. "No, not at all." He then proceeded to tell David Kendall, M.D. the whole story: him coming home from work, getting out of the car in the garage, fooling around with some of his workshop projects before he opened the door to the inside of the house to a screaming hysterical Alisa and a changed life.

Dr. Kendall was taking all of this in, scribbling in the notepad he carried with him for these occasions. He would attach these notes to the inside of Alisa's chart for his use. The nurses didn't need to see them.

"Well", he went to stand up. "Let me see if she's waking up by now- I am sure she has had plenty of time to calm down. You might want to let her know you're here- whether she can hear you or not I can't say- and then I think you should go home and get some rest. She's going to be sedated, and there is nothing you can do tonight."

Liz and Jack nodded their heads in agreement. Liz looked at the clock up on the wall of the lounge- one-ten a.m. It had been a really long day, and she would be grateful to crawl into her own bed, even if she wasn't able to get any sleep.

They followed Dr. Kendall back down the brightly-lit hall to Alisa's room. She was still sound asleep, her head cocked to the left side of her bed.

"Well", Dr. Kendall sighed, "I think it would be best if I just let Mrs. Monsfeld get a good night's sleep. I think she's knocked out for the rest of the night, or morning, however you look at it." He patted Jack on the shoulder. "I'll see you tomorrow", he said, smiling at Liz.

"See you tomorrow", Liz echoed.

"Well", Jack said, turning to Liz, "What do you think the doctor is going to find out?"

"I'm really not sure…" Liz answered, her voice trailing off.

But she was sure. She was pretty sure what Dr. David Kendall, M.D. was going to find out.

* * * * * * * * *

Doug Troland, CEO, stood in front of the plate glass window of his office, staring down at the bright lights of Baltimore. To the left was the Inner Harbor, and he could see the water glistening on this hot humid morning typical of the city.

Life sure was good. He looked around his expansive office, with its expensive mahogany furniture, leather chairs, and items from all over the world he had on display. Did it get any better than this? Somehow, he didn't think so.

He sat down in his plush leather chair in front of his computer and turned the tower on. The large clock on the wall to the left of his desk said four-forty a.m. It was extremely early for him to be starting work- he normally didn't come in until at least nine, but he just did not feel like staying in his house any longer than he had to. That sewer smell really unnerved him. He felt safe at work- that was his haven.

He got up out of his chair to go to the private spacious bathroom that was in the corner of his office, turning his monitor on as he moved away from his desk.

When he was finished washing his hands and came out, he paused. Outside of the bathroom door, something was not right. It seemed like there was a smoky haze in the air, and the smell of something burning. He looked all around his computer on his desk, and the surge protector beneath. Nothing. Maybe something was burning in the building. He flung open his office door and ran down the hall, past his secretary's desk and into the common office area. He then flipped the lights on. No smoky haze and no smell. Hmmmm... he wondered. It had to be something in his office. Maybe the computer had enough, after all.

Suddenly, he caught a glimpse in one of his employee's computer monitors of a figure running up behind him. He whirled around, his stomach jumping up into his chest. No one was there. He looked at his watch- it was already five a.m. The two people that made up the cleaning crew were due in- they came every morning Monday through Friday at five a.m. to clean the office before the first employee arrived at eight. It must have been one of them.

He shook his head and rubbed his eyes- he must have been more tired than he thought. There was nothing to be jumpy about. He was totally safe at work, wasn't he?

He started to turn around to go back into his office and froze. There it was again; this time peeking over the desk directly in front of him. All he could see was the shape of a head, and a huge one at that. But it was enough. That was no member of the cleaning crew.

Doug ran. He ran as fast as his legs could carry him into his office and slammed the door, locking it as quickly as he could. He glanced at his watch. It was only five minutes after five. He breathed a sigh of relief. He could hear the two people that made up the cleaning crew- Joe and Stella, bringing their cart into the main office area.

"Doug? You here already?" Joe called. He could see the light coming out from under Doug's door. It was very unusual for him to be there before nine.

The door opened and Doug was standing there. "Yeah, I'm here already."

"Couldn't sleep, huh?" Joe smiled as he was dusting the first row of desks outside Doug's office.

"Yeah, you could say that."

"Bummer." Joe shook his head in sympathy. Stella looked up and nodded her head in agreement.

Doug went back into his office and closed the door. He was never so glad to see Joe and Stella in his life.

He went back over to his desk and flopped down in his chair, closing his eyes and rubbing his temples. "Breathe, Doug, breathe", he whispered to himself. *You're going to be just fine, there is nothing to worry about- you are safe here at work,* he thought.

"I knew it had to be my imagination", he said to himself.

"Hih..." Doug snapped his head up, listening intently. He knew it had been a rough morning already, but he was *not* imagining the noise that he just heard, *right behind him.*

"Hih." There it was again- a half sigh, half breathless gasp. It was louder this time.

Doug rolled his chair back so fast away from his desk it almost toppled over, taking him with it. Panic was starting to flutter in his chest. He could only imagine who, or *what* was under there. Terrible images flashed away in his mind.

As hard as he tried not to, he glanced under his desk as he went to get out of his chair. Nothing. He let out all the air that had been building up in his chest as he got up and walked as fast as he could to his door. He thought it would be best if he went out into the common office area with Joe and Stella for a little while.

* * * * * * * * *

Liz stood in the shower, face upturned to the warm water flowing all over her body. She was hoping it would help her sleep, although she was wide awake.

A familiar stirring started in her secret area. It was a mixture of excitement and warmth. At twenty-four, Liz had never actually been with a man, a fact that she was extremely proud of. Sure, the temptation was there, and she had plenty of chances, even fooled around a little, but her faith was stronger. She was determined to keep herself pure for her wedding night, and wanted to marry a man who did the same.

Liz reached up and grabbed the hand held shower nozzle, turning the flow of water to "massage". The hard beating of the water felt good on her skin.

She slowly moved it down to the front of her groin, parting her legs a little. The beating of the water there felt really good.

After about a minute, she leaned up against the shower wall, moaning loudly with pleasure.

Toweling off after she was done, she whispered for forgiveness. She tried not to do it too much (usually about twice a month she caved), and she tried not to think about anything at all while she was doing it, but sometimes she just couldn't help herself. After all, it was better than going out and sleeping with a man she wasn't married to, wasn't it?

She threw on a tank top and underwear before padding into her bedroom and hopping into bed. It was now five a.m. - she had read for a little while after going home before getting into the shower. She was already starting to fall asleep as soon as her head hit the pillow.

A sizable crowd was gathered around a shaking, blubbering man sitting on top of the base of one of the support columns in Wisner's Casino and Slots. A few of them had already called management over, who, after studying this shaking, blubbering man that was talking gibberish, called 911.

Right now the crowd was gathered around him not so much to observe the excitement and try to figure out just what was going on and what he was saying, but to try to calm him down until help arrived. It didn't seem to be working too well, however- the man was almost as hysterical as when he flung open one of the bathroom doors of the casino, screaming. Not yelling, but *screaming*.

An older lady in the crowd slowly made her way over to him. She bent down in front of him, her clear blue eyes meeting his terrified brown ones.

"What is your name?" She asked.

"L-l-l-ou". He could barely get it out.

"Hi Lou, I'm Gretchen. Do you mind telling me what happened?"

Lou flinched. One of the slots five feet away from him started to flash and go "ding-ding-ding!" to try to draw someone in.

Lou started to open his mouth" slowly to answer. "H-hell c-came here tonight", he croaked, teeth chattering.

"Hell? OK…" Gretchen's blue eyes widened a little. This man needed to go to the crazy ward for sure.

"A d-de-demon, a d-demon came to get m-me!" Lou stared through Gretchen, seeing, but at the same time not seeing her.

Gretchen went to stand up, making the sign of the cross on her chest. Just in case.

A tall, light-haired man had been standing nearby apart from the crowd, trying to listen. He walked over to be next to Gretchen as she turned away from Lou.

"What's his story?" He looked over at the almost hysterical man in front of him.

"I think he's having a nervous breakdown- something about demons and hell", Gretchen was shaking her head. A stab of fear suddenly gripped the man's stomach. He stood there staring at Lou, not quite sure what to say.

"Where are they taking him?" he asked Gretchen, putting a hand on her arm.

"I'm sure to the hospital, psych ward once they determine he hasn't O.D.'d on something."

"That man doesn't need a psych ward", he half-mumbled, half-addressed Gretchen. "He needs a church. Right away."

The sandy-haired man turned to go, pulling himself away from staring at Lou. He had never seen a demon before, and never wanted to, but he was sure that was what was standing behind Lou.

The eight foot tall dark figure was directly behind Lou, one bony hand on his shoulder, the other pointing towards a slot machine.

TWO

The skinny sixteen-year-old hunched over and ran down the dark alley as fast as he could, breath coming in hard gulps, hair flying. He darted back and forth, trying to stay in the shadows. Tonight was the night.

Tonight was the night that he was going to break into some vehicles. There was a brand new neighborhood where he wanted to see what kind of treasures he could find. This neighborhood had beautiful single homes, so he figured all the occupants should have money and lots of "goodies" in their cars, shouldn't they?

He quickly found his first target- a late model Mercedes. He didn't see any alarm stickers or blinking lights on the dash or console, so he figured it was a safe bet. He grabbed his one foot long heavy duty screwdriver and started to pry the window out.

POP! It broke. Pieces of tempered glass landed on the passenger seat and floor. He slid the upper part of his body into the car, and opened the glove compartment. An owner's manual, a couple pairs of sunglasses, nothing else was to be had. He glanced over at the middle console- nothing in the cupholders. He opened it up, finding nothing but some R&B CDs, and a package of tissues.

He slid back out of the window. Good thing it was spring and it was warm out, because this was going to be a long night.

He trotted further down the dark alley to victim number two- and older model Toyota. This one didn't appear to be armed either.

He readied his screwdriver, and proceeded to pry this window open as well. He was able to get it far enough out this time to slip his arm inside and unlock the door.

Opening it, he discovered that this car had less in it than the other one- it was almost bare.

"Well, you sure do know how to pick them", he admonished himself out loud. "On to number three." If this next one was successful, it would be the final "pick" of the night.

He went further down the alley until he spotted a large pick-up sitting all by itself in the dark behind a garage. Bingo. Trucks always had something good in them. This one was not armed either.

Up came the screwdriver again to pry away the window. This time, it left a dent in the door next to the window. No matter- it wasn't any skin off his back, just something else the owner's insurance company would have to take care of.

Pop! The window got a nice big hole in it this time. Plenty of room for him to put his arm in.

He opened the door, and quietly slid into the passenger seat. There was a lot of room for him to look around.

Suddenly, headlights appeared down the alley. Someone was coming. He slid further down in the seat and held the door closed. Unless they stopped, they would not notice anything wrong.

He heard tires as they rode by and peeked up in time to see an SUV turn to go out of the alley.

Well, back to work. He didn't find anything so far but the usual car stuff: fuses, bulbs, owner's manual. There was a center console though, and he opened it. Inside, there was a tray with plenty of CDs, more bulbs and fuses, and what was that?! A set of keys.

Maybe he really did hit the jackpot this time- now he could come back later and get into the owner's house!

He grabbed the tray from the console, and slid out of the pick-up, not bothering to close the door. The battery going dead was not his problem.

His night's work done, he slipped into the shadows to head back home.

* * * * * * * * * * * * *

Alisa lay in her hospital bed, wide-eyed, listening to the busy sounds the nurses were making out in the hallway. If it wasn't for hearing them bustling around and talking, she would have completely lost it.

She would have loved for the television to have been on too, but she couldn't find the remote. There was no one else in the room but her, and her hands were strapped down.

She glanced over at the clock on the wall. There was just enough light in the room to tell that it was six a.m. She wasn't sure if Jack was coming to see her after work, or if he was going to skip the whole day and see her early. Since he was one of the top executives at his insurance firm, she suspected the latter. She still would probably have to wait until eight or nine though; she didn't think he would make it any earlier than that.

Alisa desperately wanted to go home, but at the same time, she dreaded it. She just didn't know when, or if she would ever be able to stay in that house by herself again. She felt safe right where she was for now. She couldn't say the same for her home.

With her eyes beginning to feel heavy again, Alisa started to doze off. She was just so tired from this entire ordeal.

Just then, a nurse opened the door to her room, appearing at her bedside in an instant.

"Mrs. Monsfeld, Dr. Kendall would like for you to get an MRI and CAT Scan done", she said as she lightly touched Alisa's arm.

Alisa opened her eyes slowly to address her. She was a pretty nurse, about five foot six with black hair pulled in an upsweep under her hat.

The nurse explained further. She thought that she had awakened Alisa out of her drug-induced sleep.

"Dr. Kendall wants to see if there is anything going on up there (she pointed to Alisa's head) before he decides what else he is going to do."

"A psychiatrist, you mean?" What else could "else" be?

The nurse opened her eyes wide in surprise. This was the first time Alisa actually spoke since she came in. The nurse scribbled a little note in her chart.

"Here you are; now, let's get you out of bed. If unstrap you, do you promise not to try to escape?"

Alisa looked at the nurse's name tag. Brenda Ecksend, R.N. it said.

"Nurse Ecksend, I promise", she said with a smile. *Just where would I go at ten after six in the morning?* She thought. She really didn't feel like hiding in the nearby woods- probably up a tree at that- until the staff got tired of looking for her, and then finally having to try to walk home in the dark. She could see it all over WJZ, WBAL and FOX 45 news right now- "Escaped Mental Patient Loose in Baltimore! Unarmed, may be dangerous, prone to hallucinations. Last seen with medium-length blonde hair wearing a hospital gown." She smiled at the thought.

Nurse Ecksend started unstrapping Alisa's arms from the bed. What a relief that was- her wrists beginning to get sore from the straps being so tight. Alisa didn't see the hypodermic needle Nurse Ecksend had tucked away in her nearest pocket in case she did try to escape.

"Why don't you try to use the restroom before we go downstairs?" Nurse Ecksend asked Alisa, helping her out of bed. "It may take an hour or two to get these scans done."

Alisa went into her private bathroom as Nurse Ecksend rolled a wheelchair in front of the door for her.

* * * * * * * * * * *

Jack rubbed his eyes as he poured some whole-wheat cereal into his plain white ceramic bowl.

It was about six-thirty, and he had to get ready to go to work, even if it was only for a little while. He was only planning on working a half day and then going up to the hospital.

Jack poured his milk and sighed. He prayed he didn't have too many trips to make to the hospital; hopefully Alisa would be coming home before long. He really missed her. He didn't function nearly as well being home by himself as she did. He missed the touch of her body at night; making love to her… not only that, but it was so tiring when you had to go up to the hospital every day.

Thinking about Alisa, he felt himself start to get aroused. No time for that now- he would be late for work. He had to finish getting dressed and get out of the door for his forty-minute drive.

* * * * * * * * * * *

"Here you go", Doug handed a cup of coffee each to Joe and Stella and sat down at one of the desks.

"Thanks", they said in unison.

"So, Doug, tell me, what is wrong?" Joe asked. This was the first time ever that he had seen Doug before nine a.m. and he still could not believe it. He either had a very big project, or something was not right.

"What do you mean?" Doug asked with a neutral expression on his face. He was trying his best to look and act normal- to try to hide the terror that had built up inside of him and was growing every minute.

"Well, you're never in here this early. I just want to make sure this company's not going anywhere." Stella rolled her eyes. Joe was always trying to get to the bottom of things. He should have never retired from being a detective- his brain was always working overtime.

"I just could not sleep and thought I'd catch up on all my e-mails and paperwork." Doug held up his right hand as if to swear. "Promise."

Joe raised an eyebrow, studying Doug. His detective instincts told him it was a little more than that- Doug was running from something. Nevertheless, he was the boss, so Joe was not going to pry any further.

"OK, just thought I'd ask. We were just concerned, is all." Joe took a sip of his coffee.

"Thanks, but I'm fine and so is the company", Doug smiled. That was only a half-truth. The company was more than fine- he certainly was not. "Well", he slapped his palms against the tops of his legs, "I guess I'd better start doing what I came in here early to do- work." He stood up and slowly pushed the chair under the desk. He looked at his office with dread.

"Do you want me to go ahead and clean your office next?" Joe asked. "Might as well get it done now before you get started." Joe noticed Doug's face when he looked towards his office. Stella was already starting on the other side of the room. They were there every morning, so it usually stayed pretty clean and did not take them long.

"Sure, that would be great." Doug relaxed and internally heaved a sigh of relief.

Joe smiled to himself as he walked into Doug's office. He knew Doug was scared of something in his own office, but what? Too much work? *Maybe he needs a vacation, just like the rest of us,* Joe thought.

Just as he was getting ready to dust the top of Doug's desk, he stopped short. Something was burning. He sniffed the air around him. Something burning, and rotten-like sewage.

He checked underneath Doug's desk. Nothing burning at the surge protector- all the lights were green too.

He grabbed Doug's trash can from underneath his desk as well. Empty- nothing in there to stink.

He looked behind the computer monitor on top of the desk. The wires were intact- no shorts there.

Looking around the room and following his nose, he did not see any fires or sewage- he checked Doug's private bathroom and everything looked OK.

Oh well, I guess it's just one of those things, he thought, but he'd better mention it anyway.

"Hey, Doug, you might want to think about getting an electrician and plumber to come look at your office", he said as he was pushing the cleaning cart out to the common area.

"Why? What's going on?" Doug had not had any problems at all with his equipment or bathroom.

"Well, it kind of smells in there."

Doug's stomach did a 360. "Smells?"

"Yeah, like something burning. Burning, and like a sewage pipe overflowed."

Inside, Doug wanted to run away from that building, screaming at the top of his lungs. On the outside, he just stood there, a blank expression on his face. If he didn't go back into his office, he faced a barrage of questions from Joe. Him and Stella would never believe him in a million years if he told them what he felt was really going on- the real reason why it took every ounce of his being to take one step towards that office.

He swallowed once- hard- and started to walk as normally as he could towards his office. Before he walked through though, he paused, acting like there was something wrong with the door.

Finally, he stepped through, sniffing the air. He was relieved when he didn't smell anything, and started to relax.

He pulled out his chair and sat down, moving the mouse on his computer to take off the screensaver so he could get his work started. As he began to type a reply to one of his e-mails, he saw a cup on his desk that he wanted to throw out and pushed his chair away, leaning forward to throw it into his trash can.

Just then, a disembodied head appeared right in front of his face. It had deep grooves on its forehead, and on both sides of its mouth.

It opened its mouth, and Doug could see broken yellow rotted teeth.

The only other sound that filled Doug's ears besides his own screams as he fell out of his chair was *"HIH!"*

* * * * * * * * * *

The lights were flashing by Alisa's eyes pretty quickly. In a daze, she was staring up at them from her wheelchair. Nurse Ecksend was whizzing her down the hall; getting her to the MRI room as fast as possible.

When they arrived, Alisa noticed that the MRI machine was open, not closed, and breathed a sigh of relief. She was not crazy at all about being enclosed anywhere, especially in such tight quarters as an MRI machine. *This should be a breeze,* she thought.

"OK, Mrs. Monsfeld", the technician said as he and the nurse helped Alisa out of the wheelchair. "We will need for you to lie perfectly still. If you move at all, we'll have to start over again. Have you gone to the restroom?"

"Yes." Alisa nodded at the technician. She noticed that he was extremely attractive.

"Good- let's get started. Do you want any music?" Alisa shook her head no.

They had Alisa lie down on a cushioned table with a comfortable pillow for her head. The technician pressed a couple of buttons and then went over to a computer as the big white machine whirred into action.

After about five minutes of listening to the humming of the machine, Alisa felt herself start to doze off. She fluttered her eyes, fighting to stay awake. The humming was comforting and hypnotic at the same time.

Just as Alisa started to close her eyes again, they flew open. Right in front of her face, was the figure that she saw at her house, leering at her. She started to sit up so she could back away from its eyes filled with total, complete darkness. Darkness that tried to suck her in and from which there was no return.

"Let me out of here! AAAAAHHHHHH!" she screamed, flailing her arms and legs wildly. She couldn't sit up no matter how hard she tried.

"Mrs. Monsfeld!" The technician yelled out in alarm. "What is the matter?" In no time, he was by her side, one hand on her stomach to hold her down, the other pressing the buttons on the machine.

Get me OOOOWWWWWWWTTTTT!!" Alisa hollered in a guttural voice. The figure had not left- it was still hovering over her, its dark soulless pits for eyes burning holes into her retinas.

* * * * * * * * *

The skinny sixteen-year-old was finding it hard to concentrate on his schoolwork.

It wasn't because he was tired- no, he'd had plenty of nights staying up until two a.m. breaking into autos and then going through his loot after getting it back home; he just felt "off". It seemed to him that ever since he woke up like he had a dark cloud hanging over his head and he wasn't sure why.

Actually, when he really thought about it, the feeling started the night before. On his way home he felt like someone, or something, was following him. He shook it off as paranoia, even though everything in the neighborhood he hit was totally dark and he was positive nobody saw him.

He shook his head to try to clear it. He was just trying to do too much lately. What with school, a part-time job, a girlfriend, and his "side" job of breaking into autos, he was extremely busy. That and he had broken into at least fifteen of them the past two weeks alone. He was just tired, that was all.

"Robby." A cute, red-haired girl bounded up alongside of him. "Hey, where are you going in such a hurry?" The bell had rang, and Robby was out in the hall walking to his next class.

"Sorry, Karen, I was just trying to get to calculus."

Karen looked up at him with bright green eyes. "Yeah, right, since when have you been in a hurry to get to any class?" She smirked at him as she grabbed his arm.

He looked down at her with a sullen glance, which made her stop and take a step back. "Are you alright?" She asked, her heart starting to pound. Normally, he was glad to see her, or when they hung out, joked around a lot and was pretty much always in a good mood. She'd never seen this look on his face before. She hoped that she didn't get that "we need to talk" speech.

"I'll talk to you later, babe", he said, walking into his math class. Something was really bothering him- he didn't even look back.

* * * * * * * *

Liz glanced at her alarm clock by her bed as she pulled an outfit from her closet- it was eight-thirty already. She was really surprised she slept that late, considering the night she had and worrying about Alisa.

Worrying about Alisa was nothing new, however. She had always worried about Alisa since they were kids sleeping on the rotten wooden floor of their small ranch house.

Worrying about Alisa when she would bear the brunt of their father and mother's anger. Worrying about Alisa when she ran away from home when Liz was twelve and Alisa was fifteen.

Swinging her legs out of bed and rubbing her eyes, she was starting to wake up. She figured she'd at least check in at work and let her boss know that she would need to be out most of the day. He wasn't much of a sympathetic person, but surely he would understand her need to make sure her sister was alright. After all, he did have a wife- even though it was an ex-wife- and kids- he must know what it was like to worry about someone he cares about at least one time in his life.

She threw on a simple satin blouse and black dress pants, combed her hair, smoothed the sheets and bedspread out, and made her way downstairs. She was due in at work at nine, so she decided to take her breakfast to go. She grabbed a bagel and cream cheese and headed out the door.

* * * * * * *

Jack had only been at work for thirty minutes, but he had already composed a memo and answered ten e-mails. He was on a roll this morning.

He figured he would take care of one more memo and call it a day already. He really was anxious to get up to the hospital- he didn't think Alisa was at the point yet where she would be OK for long without him or Liz there with her. Let his secretary take care of the letters to his clients that he had to write today- that's what she was there for.

He finished the memo, e-mailed it out, and shut his computer down. He would probably be at the hospital in a half hour.

* * * * * * *

Joe and Stella had just finished cleaning the office common area and were getting ready to get into the elevator when they heard the loud screams. They looked at each other in surprise. Those screams were coming from Doug's office. Then, just as soon as they started, they abruptly stopped. Stella grabbed Joe's arm as they ran towards Doug's office.

"Joe..." Stella was wide-eyed as she stared at Doug's door- it was closed. She was anxious to check it out, but at the same time dreaded to see what she might find on the other side.

Joe knew what she was thinking. "Stella, we're up on the tenth floor. If anyone was going to get through Doug's windows, they'd have to use a window-washer platform, and then break his window- they don't open. Not only that, it's reinforced tempered glass. They'd almost need a jackhammer to break one of those things. Unless...unless they decided to crawl all the way through the vents."

Stella thought either scenario was highly unlikely. Nevertheless...

"Why don't you..." she said as Joe grabbed a towel from their cleaning cart and inched his way towards Doug's door. He really, really wished he had his gun on him right now.

Finally, he made it to Doug's door. Wrapping the towel around his hand, he slowly turned the handle which was unlocked, and opened the door just slightly. If there was an intruder inside, he didn't want to alarm them right away

Peeking inside, he looked around the room as much as he could. He didn't see anything amiss or anyone around; not even Doug.

He flung the door open, and walked inside. His instincts were screaming that something was horribly, desperately wrong. He caught a faint whiff of a sulfur smell when he reached the center of the room, and frowned. It was almost like the same smell as before, but different. He looked around- nothing.

He turned around to the left of him and walked over to Doug's private bathroom. Opening that door, he stepped in and looked around. He was always still amazed when he was in Doug's bathroom. It was beautiful, with nice ceramic floors, a marble countertop and sink, a big round mirror, and brushed nickel fixtures. It even had a nice shower. The perks of the executives...

Noting nothing unusual in there, he walked out, still clutching the towel. He was no longer a member of a cleaning crew. He was a detective who came out of retirement. It felt good.

He went back to the center of the room and stood there, head cocked to one side. Out of the corner of his eye he could see Stella standing outside of the door. She was not too close, but not so far away that she couldn't lend a helping hand if needed. Hearing nothing, he started walk around the right side of Doug's desk, and that is when he let out a gasp.

Sticking out halfway from underneath Doug's desk, with the chair pushed back was the body of a man- from the waist down. Joe didn't have to turn the body over so he could see the face to know that it was Doug.

Grabbing his cell phone and walking out of the office, he dialed 911.

"Well, what happened?" Stella asked when he hung up.

"It's Doug."

"Is he..."

"Yes."

"Why? How could that have happened??!" Stella was crying now, her voice started to come in breaks.

"I don't know hon, I just don't know", Joe said as he hugged Stella tight to his chest.

THREE

Rob lay sideways on his bed, half-heartedly doing his math homework. He didn't really feel like doing anything at all except sleeping. He didn't even feel like seeing Karen.

He couldn't quite put his finger on it, but he just didn't feel right. Not physically, but mentally. Maybe he was depressed. Yeah, that was it.

Suddenly, the door opened, and Karen came bouncing in. She jumped next to him on his bed enthusiastically, knocking his calculus book to the floor.

"Karen!" He exclaimed, letting out a harsh sigh.

"Sor-r-y. Don't be so uptight", she smiled as she rolled over on her back. "What's the matter with you, anyway?" She grabbed his chin and stared deep into his dark brown eyes, which were dull and lifeless- not full of laughter like they usually were. "And don't tell me 'nothing'".

"I really don't know what it is, Karen, I think I've just been studying too much."

Karen let out a snort. "You can't be serious!" She laughed as she rolled around on the bed, clutching her stomach.

"I'm serious, Karen", he frowned at her. "I'm tired, and I just don't feel like doing anything but sleeping."

Karen reached out and smoothed his straight black hair back from his forehead. "OK then, I'll see you tomorrow. Go get some good sleep." She got up and went to walk out.

"Karen?" He called as she was getting ready to close his door. She turned around and looked at him, red hair flying and green eyes flashing.

"I'll be better tomorrow, I promise."

She smiled. "Good night."

"Love you, Karen."

"Love you, Robby." She closed his door behind her as she blew him a kiss and walked out of his room.

He closed his eyes as he rubbed his forehead. He couldn't even tell Karen what was really going on. She didn't know what his "hobby" was at night, and he was so grateful that she was not one to be possessive and ask a lot of questions.

He couldn't tell her that he just didn't feel right after breaking into that pickup truck last night.

* * * * * * * * * * * * *

Liz sat her things down at her desk, and started to walk over to her boss's office.

"He's not here today", his secretary, Betty called over to her as she walked by. "He's in the hospital."

Liz walked over to her, a surprised look on her face. Her boss hardly ever missed a day's work, unless he decided to take a rare day off for one of his kid's school functions.

"*Hospital?!*" She exclaimed. "What in the world happened? It had to be something brought on by stress. *He takes this place way too serious,* she thought.

"Not sure, all I know is that he was at the casinos in Delaware yesterday, and they took him to the hospital from there. He's supposed to have been transferred to North General by now."

"That's the same hospital my sister is in- I came in today to let him know that I would be up there with her all day."

"I'll mark you down as excused, Liz, don't worry about it", Betty said. "What's wrong with Alisa?"

"She had a nervous breakdown, I think", Liz replied. "Her husband came home to find her hysterical for some reason or other." Liz only told Betty this because she knew she could trust her. Everything she ever told her always stayed just between the two of them.

A thoughtful look crossed Betty's face.

"That's funny", she said, "That's almost the same thing that happened to Lou. I had spoken with his ex-wife, and she said that he had some kind of breakdown in the casino and they had to sedate him to get him in the ambulance. I hope he's OK to where they're not going to keep him in the mental ward. That's a horrible place."

"I hope so, too", Liz said and she meant it. Lou and she had their differences from time to time, but she never wanted to see anything bad happen to anyone, regardless of how they treated her. "I'd better go. I plan on coming in tomorrow or Wednesday", Liz continued as she started back to her desk.

"OK, Liz, you take it easy, we'll see you later", Betty called.

As she was collecting her purse and coat from her desk and walking out of the office, she was thinking how strange things were getting. What were the odds that two people she knew would have nervous breakdowns one right after the other?

She hurried out to the parking lot and into her car. She really had to find out what happened to Alisa, and she needed to find out today.

* * * * * * * * * * *

Joe held Stella as tightly to his chest as he could while he watched the action that was taking place in Doug's office.

The paramedics got to work right away after they arrived. Joe watched from the office common area as they carefully pulled his lifeless body out from under his desk, and was concerned when he saw the frowns come over their faces after they turned him onto his back.

He knew before they started performing CPR and defibrillating Doug that he was dead and not coming back. Stella knew it too, because that's when she started to cry. It wasn't loud, racking sobs, but a silent cry- the kind that you do when you don't want to call attention to yourself.

Joe gave Stella a squeeze and rubbed her back. Tears were still streaming down her cheeks. Joe felt his eyes well up with tears as well, but he was determined not to break down. Not now.

He glanced at the clock on the wall behind him. It was only 7:10 which was good. The first employee came in at 8:00, and was rarely early. At least Doug's body should be out of the office by then. It was going to be upsetting enough for everyone without having to see their boss' body and a young boss at that.

His thoughts turned towards Doug's family. We wondered how they would ever get through this. Especially his little girl...

He was jerked back to the present by a detective's voice- one that he knew well. "Hey Joe", Jerry Johnson said as he clapped him one on the arm. "How you been, man? I bet it seems almost like old times, doesn't it?"

Joe and J.J. had worked together on a number of cases, and had gotten along extremely well. They could always talk to one another about anything, which was good. J.J. was going to be the lead detective on this case, so he was going to be conducting most of the interviews. He still had about four more years and then he could retire.

He stood in front of Joe and Stella, a serious look on his face- the look of police business.

"Sammy is on his way to pick up the body", he said. Sammy was one of the coroners who they always called when they had a "pick-up". "He should be here any minute now." He knew what Joe was thinking, so he continued. "We have a detective on her way to notify the family as we speak. Can I ask you a few questions?"

"Sure, no problem", Joe replied. He proceeded to tell J.J. everything he knew, from how he thought it was odd that Doug was in the office so early in the morning, to the screams he heard from Doug's office. "It was almost like he was running from someone...or *something*", Joe finished.

Just as soon as J.J. was through asking his questions, Sammy was getting ready to wheel out Doug's body. J.J. stopped him and his assistant at the entrance to Doug's office door and motioned Joe over. Stella walked up behind him and stood at his side.

"I think you should take a look at this", he said. Joe had been around J.J. long enough to know what that meant, and it was never anything good. "Let me know what you think. To be honest, I don't know what to make of it- I've never seen anything like it before." He unzipped the body bag enough to show down to the top of Doug's torso.

As soon as the bag was opened and Joe could see in, he took a step back and gasped, holding his chest. He felt like he was going to pass out for sure. Never in all of his years of police work did he see anything like this.

Stella jumped and let out a small scream, making the sign of the cross as she did so. The sight that both of them saw was going to haunt them for a long time to come.

Doug had looked like he aged fifty years. A series of long, deep lines made their way on his forehead and down each cheek next to his mouth. He had lost most of his light brown hair. What was left on his head was a single dingy off- brown puffball.

With his mouth still open from his last scream, they could see crooked rotten yellow-brown teeth.

* * * * * * * *

Alisa slowly opened her eyes to find herself back in her hospital room, strapped to the bed again. Nurse Ecksend was by her side, watching her.

"Good, you're awake", she said. "Dr. Kendall is on his way to see you- he should be here in about fifteen minutes. Is there anything I can get you?" She asked.

"Yeah", Alisa said wearily, "a bible."

Without saying another word, Nurse Ecksend opened the drawer in the night stand next to Alisa's bed and placed the bible on her stomach. Alisa's hands could move just enough to open it and go to the pages she wanted, which she had no idea where to start.

Nurse Ecksend walked out of the room, telling Alisa she would be back tomorrow, her shift was almost over.

Alisa opened the bible to Genesis. She figured the beginning was as good a place as any to start. Maybe she could understand sooner or later what was happening to her and why she was being "visited" by this entity or whatever it was called. She really needed to speak to Liz right now.

She got to the third chapter when she felt someone watching her. Looking up, she saw Jack in the doorway.

"Hey hon", she looked up, smiling at him in relief.

"Glad to see you finally awake", he replied. He looked down at the bible on her lap. "What is this? Are you becoming like Liz now?" He teased, rubbing her thigh which was under the covers.

"I don't know if that's such a bad thing", Alisa answered.

Liz was walking down the fifth floor hall of North General, on her way to Alisa's room again. She really hoped her sister was awake today- they desperately needed to talk.

As she was scanning the rooms for Alisa's number, a voice croaked out at her from room 519.

"Liz", it called.

She stopped walking and whirled around to face the room and the voice. Looking in, she saw that it was Lou. He was strapped down to the bed as well, eyes wide, hair wild, looking like a frightened, caged animal.

"I knew you were up here at the hospital", Liz said as she walked in, "I just didn't know what floor." Liz didn't want to embarrass him or get Betty in trouble for telling.

"Yeah, they put me in the crazy ward for some reason", Lou replied.

Liz could tell he didn't want to be alone. She was really anxious to get to Alisa, but she didn't know she was coming up that early anyway. She pulled up one of the chairs in the corner next to Lou's bed.

"Liz, it looks like you were right about this hell stuff all along", he said as she sat down. His frightened eyes searched hers, pleading.

"What are you talking about?" Liz frowned.

"Hell is real- I believe you now", he said softly.

Liz's mind flashed back to an incident at work one day, during her lunch break. She was sitting at her desk reading the bible and looking up biblical facts on the internet when Lou walked by.

"You know, there's no room for that inappropriate stuff at the workplace", he said snidely. "Don't you get all preachy with us around here."

To that, Liz looked at him and cocked up one eyebrow. "Lou, if there's no room for God in the workplace then just where is He supposed to be? You know, sometimes work is where we need Him the most. He's the only thing that's permanent in a temporary world."

"Yeah, OK", he waved his hand in dismissal, inwardly groaning as he started to walk away. "All that stuff's not real, anyway."

Liz snapped back into the present. She figured now was not the time to tell him 'I told you so'. She supposed he already knew that anyway. He was scared and looking for answers.

"What happened, Lou?" She finally asked him.

He noticeably flinched in his bed. "If I don't tell you now, I never will", he replied. "I *never* want to relive that again- *ever*." He could barely get the words out. "I saw hell itself", he said with wide eyes.

Liz leaned in closer towards Lou. She had never known anyone who had seen hell before, or at least talked about it, anyway. This was really getting interesting.

"Liz, you know I have *never* entertained even the thought of that stuff before, so you do believe what I am getting ready to tell you, don't you?" He asked.

She nodded.

"Well, when I was at the casino yesterday and visited the bathroom, that was when it started." He paused to get a drink of water that was next to his bed and swallowed, hard.

"It started as a black haze that filled the room, almost like a thick black smoke. At first, I thought maybe I was ready to pass out, and then I smelled the sulfur; I guess what everyone always calls 'fire and brimstone.' After that, I saw a demon- one of those reaper looking things that you see at Halloween."

Liz smiled and nodded.

"It looked just like one of those things except when it pulled its hood back, it had eyes. They were eyes just like yours and mine, except the retina part was all black-hollow and soulless. When it looked straight at you, it was looking straight *into* you. Know what I mean?"

"Yes." Liz could barely choke the words out. She was on the edge of her seat. She knew though, that no matter how vividly Lou described what happened, it would never match actually *living* through it and being able to come back.

Lou continued, his voice becoming more animated. He kept glancing out into the hall to make sure no nurses were coming his way. Surely if they heard him, they would sedate him to where he would not be able to tell any more of his "tales."

"And when it looked into me, I could feel a total, complete hatred. I knew what it was thinking and feeling. It *wanted* me to know. It didn't say anything at all, but I just knew. It wanted me to stay there with it, but at the same time it completely and totally hated me. It wanted to hurt me as much as possible, to break me completely down, over and over again." Lou took another sip of his water. "After it stared at me for awhile, it motioned for me to follow it. Then, it pointed behind it, where there was a slot machine, and a fire burning behind that. By this time the room was getting pretty hot. After I saw that, I took off out of the bathroom. Next thing I remember, I was in the ambulance. I know some people were talking to me, but I don't remember what they said. I was trying to forget what happened and at the same time, not able to get it out of my mind. The EMT in the ambulance had asked me what had happened, to make me have a 'psychotic episode' as he put it. I lied and told him I don't know, maybe all the slot machines set me off." Lou smiled at this little bit of cleverness. "Could you see that now? I'd never be able to go home in a million years if I told that guy the truth."

Liz nodded. It was sad but true. Many, many people believed in heaven and hell, but at their convenience- as a faraway place, accessible only by death. Little did they know, unless they found out like Lou, just how close both of them *really* were.

"That's why I was really anxious to tell you, Liz", he said. "I knew that you were the only one I could tell what really happened. I knew that you would understand and believe me- that you would know I wasn't having some kind of delusion."

"You're right, Lou, I understand completely." She stopped at that. She knew that now was definitely not the time for a "sermon". She really thought about telling him that she was glad he understood too, and that he now believed what she had been trying to tell him all along: that this "religious stuff" was one hundred percent real, and that she guessed he now felt it was "appropriate" to talk about it. That always got her. What in the world ever gave people the audacity to even think that it was "inappropriate" to talk about the Lord?? How *dare* they!!

Snapping back to the present, she stood up to go- she really had to see how Alisa was doing. Something was telling her she needed to get to her room pretty quickly.

"Are you leaving me?" Lou asked. "I really wish you could stay, but I guess I have to deal with this by myself sometime."

"You're never alone if you have Jesus in your heart. He'll always be with you." Liz gave him a warm smile.

"Liz, what do I do now? How can I ensure that I never go to hell? I never ever want to experience that again and I just got a tiny glimpse of it, let alone forever." His eyes were wide.

"Here, take two of these." Liz whipped out a tract from her purse- she always had at least one handy. "Also, read the bible- I know there should be one in your drawer over there." She pointed to the table next to his bed. "We'll talk more tomorrow- I'll be by then."

"Thanks, Liz, you don't know how much this means to me", he said as she was leaving.

She looked back at Lou. "Don't mention it", she said. Every soul she could bring to the Lord was her pleasure.

* * * * * * *

Joe walked out into his kitchen to see Stella sitting at the island drinking a cup of tea. Noticing Joe, she said, "I couldn't sleep."

"I can't sleep no more, either", he said, flopping down on a stool.

"I just can't get it out of my mind what happened today. Joe, I'm scared."

He grabbed her hand. "I know, I know. Everything is going to be OK."

"What do you think caused that?"

"Hon, I don't know, but I don't think it might have been of this world."

Stella shuddered, even over the warmth of her tea. She was surprised that Joe mentioned something like that. He always had a 'logical' explanation for everything. "Joe, I don't think I can go back in that building, let alone near that office."

He grabbed her hand and gave it a light squeeze. If what happened today haunted them so bad, he couldn't imagine how his wife and little girl would take it the first time they saw someone they *thought* they knew. He was sure that would haunt them the rest of their lives, as it was more than likely going to do to Stella and him. He still felt really bad for allowing Doug to go back into that office, when it was obvious to him that something was keeping Doug from wanting to go in there.

"Joe, you don't think it's contagious, do you?" Stella looked scared half to death.

"I don't think so, honey." He squeezed her hand again. Her face was as pale as a tombstone bathed in the moonlight of a winter's night. Her face looked just like he felt- sallow and washed out.

Thinking about it, Joe couldn't be sure that it *wasn't* contagious. Just because he'd never seen something like that during all his years on the force didn't mean that it wasn't out there- somewhere. He figured he had about two days and then he could get a copy of the coroner's report from Jerry. Hopefully it would be able to ease Stella's mind- and his.

* * * * * *

Rob finished his breakfast, told his dad to have a good day, gave his mom a kiss on the cheek, grabbed his books and walked out the front door to go to school. It usually only took him about twenty minutes to get there, but he was going to take his time this morning. He still felt "off". He thought maybe he was doing too much, so it was time to take it easy. Walking to school at a slower pace was a good way to start.

He purposefully walked another route (and a longer one at that) this morning. He was hoping that none of his friends, or Karen for that matter, had the same idea. He needed to take time this morning to think. What was wrong with him? He normally wanted to spend as much time as possible with Karen, but didn't feel like doing that today. He always enjoyed walking to school with her and his friends; laughing, joking, and smoking cigarettes but he didn't feel like doing that either. He normally always looked at the cars as he walked by each morning to see which ones had "goodies" in them and make mental notes to come back to them later, but this morning was different- not even a glance. Something was definitely up. Ever since he broke into that pickup...

It was too late to return the goods now. The owner was more than likely on the lookout; and the warpath. His only other option was to throw his bounty away and try to forget about it. That's just what he was going to do when he got home.

When he got to school, he didn't see any of his friends or Karen standing outside. He figured they must have already went in and he breathed a sigh of relief. After all, he arrived about ten minutes later than he usually did.

He put his stuff away in his locker and slipped behind his desk at homeroom.

"Hi, Rob, what's up?" The big kid that sat in front of him, Chris Sandeson, had known that he came in and turned around to say hi. Chris was OK- not real tall, about fifty pounds overweight, and never wore the latest hairstyle for his medium-brown hair, or the latest clothes, but he always tried to make people laugh. And that was important.

"Hey Chris, what's up?" Rob gave him a smile. The bell then rang, and Chris quickly turned back around to face the front of the room.

As the homeroom teacher was making some morning announcements, Rob felt someone lay their hand on his shoulder. He spun around, worried that it might be the vice-principal or the principal himself. Had they found him out?

There was no one behind him, only the back wall of the classroom.

He felt a hand, he just knew he did. He ran his hands through his short spiky hair. He guessed he really needed to get some sleep. It probably was his muscle twitching from lack of it, or maybe he was laying in his bed the wrong way.

The announcements were now over, and the morning bell rang to signal to everyone that it was time to go to the first class. Rob touched his shoulder and got butterflies in his stomach- it was burning hot. *What in the world??* He thought. He still felt the pressure of the hand on his shoulder, too.

He started looking for Karen in the hall. Usually they met halfway and walked together to their morning class, which was right next to one another. She was his beacon of sanity.

He was almost to his first class, and she was nowhere to be found. *Oh well*, he thought, *maybe she's giving me more space.*

A few more hours, a few more classes, and it was lunch time. He did not feel the hand on his shoulder again. He grabbed his lunch, which was in a plain brown bag, out of his locker and walked down the hall to the cafeteria. He saw a few of his friends sitting at a table not far from the entrance where he walked in, so he went over to join them and plopped down.

"Hey guys", he said. They were all on the football team with him, and they usually sat together every day at lunch- one of the many "jock" tables in the cafeteria.

He was starting to relax; laughing and joking with his buddies, when all of a sudden he felt another hand on his shoulder. Spinning around, there really was someone behind him this time. It was Don Odewell- one of the school nerds who happened to be in most of Rob's classes. Don was almost in every club imaginable at the school. He was very gifted and smart, but somehow just didn't fit in with the "cool" crowd. He had brains, but lacked the social skills to interact with people to where they wouldn't feel he was "weird".

"What is it, Don?" Rob tried to ask him as nicely as possible. He figured plenty of other kids gave him a hard enough time as it was.

Don bent down close enough to have his mouth almost on Rob's left ear and whispered: "I know what it is you've been doing most nights to cars and stuff. You'd better talk to Kevin before principal Caswell knows, too." He then walked away, leaving Rob sitting at the table in a stupor, butterflies flying frantically around in his stomach.

"Hey Rob- yo!" His buddy Diante was snapping his fingers in front of his face, forcing him to come back to the present. "You okay? What did he say to you, man- do we have to get him? You haven't touched your lunch yet- we only have fifteen minutes left. You looked like your dog just died or something, man."

"I'm OK", Rob said, grabbing his pack and slinging it over his shoulder. "I gotta go." He left the guys to fight over his lunch.

He had to find Kevin, and fast.

FOUR

"Dr. Kendall, I want to go home", Alisa told him as soon as he walked into her room.

He pulled up a chair, sat down and looked over at Jack, who was already on his way out. "Give us about a half hour, OK?" He asked.

Then, looking over at Alisa, he said, "Tell me what reason I would have to release you. We really don't have any intention of keeping you here forever, but we don't want to release you without knowing what is going on." He gazed at her steadily. "Can you tell me what exactly is going on? I heard about the incident in the MRI."

Alisa stared back at him. "If I told you, you'd never believe me."

"I can't tell you how many times I've heard that one. I don't think there's anything out there I *haven't* heard." His notepad and pen were resting on his lap, waiting for his latest notes."

"If I tell you, do you promise not to keep me here against my will?" Alisa still really wanted to go home. She didn't know much about psychiatry, but she had enough knowledge to realize that there was nothing they could do for her particular situation. The only person she knew for sure that could help her was Liz.

Dr. Kendall raised an eyebrow. "I'm waiting", he said.

"Well, I keep seeing a figure", Alisa said nervously. She was scared as it was, and Dr. Kendall made her even more nervous with his good looks.

"Okay. What kind of figure?" Dr. Kendall started scribbling away in his notepad.

"A very dark figure, with a tattered robe and even darker black eyes, like soulless eyes. It just stares at me, and tries to move closer, ever closer..." Alisa's voice trailed off and she got a distant look in her eyes.

"Hmmm..." Dr. Kendall scribbled some more in his notepad.

"Sounds like you're seeing a demon to me, Alisa," Liz popped her head around the doorway, an excited expression on her face. This was the first time she was hearing anything from Alisa herself.

Dr. Kendall looked up from his notes to give a slight smile to Liz. *Not again*, he groaned inwardly. There had to be one of those in every family- one of those "religious fanatics". He couldn't knock them for trying, but sometimes it wore on his nerves having to endure their take of what was going on. For the most part, they agreed with what he was doing and thought therapy and medication were the answer, but there were always those few... and he believed that Liz was one of them. One of them who was never satisfied with what science had to say about a particular situation. She really was an attractive girl, though...

"Could you give us some more time?" He asked Liz. "Maybe come back in about twenty minutes." He looked at his watch.

"Certainly", she smiled. He watched her light blonde hair flip as she turned away to walk down the hall.

Turning back to Alisa, he asked, "Now, tell me, how many times so far have you seen this 'figure'?"

Alisa suddenly had a horrified look on her face. "I- I'm s-s-s-seeing it n-n-now."

Dr. Kendall scribbled some more in his notes. He looked up for her to continue.

"It's right next to you." She pointed to his right side.

Dr. Kendall's stomach suddenly dropped. He was scared to look over. He had been through this kind of thing many times before, but now it just seemed different. He couldn't quite put his finger on it, but he did not feel that Alisa had anything wrong with her mentally. She just did not exhibit any of the other classic signs of schizophrenia, which most people would automatically think she had.

His suspicions were confirmed in a split second. Out of the corner of his eye, he saw a dark figure on his right side. A feeling of dread and anxiety automatically overcame him and a sick feeling spread throughout his stomach. His mind started swirling with all kinds of horrible thoughts, mashed together like a lump of potatoes. He wanted to try to act like nothing was going on, but it was too late. Alisa saw his eyes move over to where the figure stood.

"Do you see what I mean now? Do you?" Her voice was almost steady this time.

Dr. Kendall felt it more than he saw it. More than anything, he wanted to jump up and run out of that room, away from Alisa and away from the dark figure. "Yes, I believe you, Alisa." Those were the only words that he could get out of his mouth. He swallowed once, hard. He was starting to break out in a cold sweat and needed to get up and walk around. He needed to get out of that room. "If you'll excuse me."

Jack suddenly appeared in the doorway. Summoning the strength to address him, Dr. Kendall said, "I will speak with both of you sometime tomorrow, okay?" He then quickly walked down the hall, leaving Jack to stare after him in bewilderment. He had to put as much distance as possible between him and that room. It wasn't until he was about five hundred feet away that the feeling of anxiety, dread and sickness passed, and his head cleared.

* * * * * * * * * * * * *

"Stella, I'll be back in a little while." Joe gave her a hug and a kiss and grabbed his car keys.

She knew where he was headed. He was going down to the city morgue to see if he could find out what *really* happened. She wasn't expecting him back any time soon.

She knew that old habits die hard, and Joe was not going to give up until every lead was followed; every question answered.

Joe hopped in his car and headed down to the morgue as fast as he could. With his many years on the force, he had developed a very close working relationship and friendship with the M.E., Francis McDowell. Those two had collaborated on many a case together; sometimes spending more time with each other in the morgue studying the causes of death than living with their own families.

Joe pulled around to one of the rear entrances of the hospital, and walked over to a staircase leading down. That was the direct entrance to the basement, and the morgue, although it was not marked.

He opened the door and walked down the dimly lit hallway until he came to a door on his left. It was simply marked with a small "morgue" sign next to it.

He turned the door handle and walked on in. "Frank?" he called.

"Back here", a muffled voice answered. "How've you been, Joe??" Frank stood up and gave Joe a big hug and a clap on the back.

"It's great to see you, although I admit, I'm not surprised. J.J. told me you were there." Frank nodded towards one of the tables in the middle of the room. "I figured you'd be here sometime tonight."

"Have you found out anything yet?" Joe asked anxiously.

"Haven't even started. Been waiting for you, actually." Frank smiled. "Shall we?" He walked over to the table directly in the middle of the room, and flung the sheet back. The body of Doug Troland lay there: naked, eyes closed, a small white towel covering his groin.

Even though Joe had last seen Doug not even twenty-four hours ago, he stepped back a little at the sight of his body again. It was still a shock to see his former boss this way.

"I know what you're thinking, Joe, and no; I've never seen anything like this before. There's no body that's ever come through this morgue that had aged forty to fifty years right at the moment of death."

"You don't think this is some kind of disease, do you?" Joe asked, still keeping one eye on Doug's lifeless body. Joe almost expected that at any minute, Doug was going to jump up off the table- lunging at the both of them- trying to rip them up with those rotten yellow teeth.

"Hardly", Frank replied as he was making a Y-shaped incision down Doug's chest, "I am pretty sure even a bio-terrorism weapon couldn't do anything like this."

Frank yanked back the flaps of skin left from the incision and started to cut away at the breast-bone with a grinder. It made a loud whining "yeee-ah" noise.

Once cut, he pried the ribcage open, stopping before going any further. His mouth flew open behind his mask.

Joe attended enough of these to know when Frank felt something was not quite right, and now was one of those times.

"What's going on?" He asked him.

Frank pulled his mask down to his chin and set the grinder on the table.

"Didn't you say that you found him in his office under his desk?" He asked Joe.

Joe stepped a little closer to the table. "Yeah, that's right; he was under the desk crunched up in a ball- that's how I found him."

Frank motioned for Joe to come closer. "Take a look at this. Unbelievable."

Joe stepped up next to the table, looked down and gasped. He didn't really know what organ was what, but it didn't matter. Almost all of them were unrecognizable; ninety-five percent burned on all but a few. He looked up at Frank.

"Joe, I have absolutely *no* explanation for this. It looks like someone barbecued his insides. As you can see, it's not chemical. It would be a different type of burn- mostly internal, and what would show on the outside would make it look raw- not charred." He touched one of the organs, the liver, with the tip of his scalpel. A sheet of black ash fell off of it into cavern of his stomach. "Good Lord", Frank breathed.

Joe just stood there shell-shocked. It was bad enough to find his boss the way he did. The next thing was seeing how he looked when they placed him on the gurney. But now having this surprise after he was opened up… Joe thought he could have possibly seen it all now. He was mentally preparing himself for many sleepless nights to come.

* * * * * * * * * * * *

Rob ran down the hall as quickly as he could with fists clenched looking for Kevin Hughes. He would have never believed that Kevin was a snitch.

Hundreds of thoughts were racing through his mind at a mile a minute. How did Kevin know what he was up to at night? Rob and he were not that close of buddies. Furthermore, how could *anyone* have known? He was so careful; always making sure no one was around. Not only that, but he never told anyone what it was that he did, or what it was that he "bought" lately. Everyone would be suspicious if he showed them, a new gotten treasure every couple of days or so.

He strode up to where Kevin's locker was and stopped, deciding to wait and see if he came to it before classes started again.

Kevin Hughes was just a regular guy. He didn't hang out with the jocks, but he wasn't a nerd, either. He really didn't fit in with any one particular clique at all. He had friends from all different crowds, and Don Odewell was one of them. In fact, he hung out with Don the most. It made sense that anything he knew, Don was going to know as well. But, how *did* he know? Rob rubbed his forehead on that one.

The five-minute bell suddenly rang- time to head to class. Rob guessed that Kevin wasn't going to make a stop at his locker after all. Oh well. There would be later. Until then, the question on Rob's mind was going to eat at him.

* * * * * * * * * * *

Liz walked into the entrance of North General hospital, clutching a large yellow envelope in her right hand. It was only six-twenty p.m., so she had plenty of time- visiting hours were over at eight-thirty.

She wanted to come up later in the day so maybe she could see if there was any more information from Dr. Kendall. She had planned on visiting Alisa first and then popping in to see Lou.

Walking into Room 510, she was very happy to see that Alisa was up and looking towards the door. Upon seeing Liz walk in, she broke into a huge smile.

"Hey, baby sis", she said. She was extremely bubbly- Liz was normally the enthusiastic one.

"Hey 'Lise, what's up?" Liz pulled up one of the chairs that was against the wall and sat down next to the bed, grabbing one of Alisa's hands and giving it a squeeze.

"Guess what? Dr. Kendall said he is releasing me tomorrow."

Liz let out a hoot. "Hallelujah!! That's great!"

"Jack was already here. He'll be back about one o'clock tomorrow to pick me up."

"That's wonderful. Did Dr. Kendall say anything else to you?"

"No… he just came in for about a minute with his notepad and told me he was releasing me tomorrow. Then he left."

"Hmmm… interesting. I am going to see if I can find out anything before I check in on Lou. I'll be by tomorrow after you get home, OK?"

"OK", Alisa said.

"See you then", Liz said, kissing her on the cheek. She turned around and waved to Alisa on her way out of the room.

Coming out of Alisa's room, Dr. Kendall almost knocked her down.

"I am so sorry, Ms. Pearson", he said. "How are you?"

"I'm fine, Dr. Kendall. Do you have a minute? I'd like to talk to you about Alisa."

"Sure, let's go into my office." He led the way down the hall to a door off to the left. Going in, it was a large sized room, nicely decorated with potted plants and trees, various small paintings, and his certificates and licenses.

He motioned to one of the chairs in front of his desk. "Have a seat", he said.

"Dr. Kendall, I found out that you are releasing Alisa tomorrow. Do you think that is a good idea? Has she been 'cured' already?"

"Ms. Pearson, what I will tell you is that there is no cure for what she has. The MRI came out normal, what we could get of it. I don't really believe it, but what she is experiencing is not of this world."

Liz couldn't believe what she was hearing. Doctors didn't believe in that sort of thing, did they? They only believed in what science had to tell them. Surely this couldn't be the only explanation Dr. Kendall had for her.

Dr. Kendall saw the incredulous look on Liz's face. "Just make sure she gets plenty of rest. You'll be looking in on her, won't you?"

"Yes", Liz replied. Now that she knew Alisa was coming home, she planned on taking the rest of the week off to be with her during the day while Jack had to work. She didn't think Alisa would be ready to be home by herself just yet. Not only that, but they still needed to talk about what happened.

Liz's mind was still ticking. She was trying to find a reason to keep the conversation going on with Dr. Kendall for a while. She was happy, but at the same time a little disappointed that Alisa was going home so soon. She was honestly going to miss seeing Dr. Kendall a little. He was *so* good-looking. She might have to see if she could check in a few days herself.

Dr. Kendall noticed the far-away look in Liz's eyes. "Are you OK?" He asked.

"Yes, I am- thanks. I just was thinking about if I had any more questions or not." She stood up to leave.

Dr. Kendall crossed the room over to her, placing a hand on her arm. "Alisa will be just fine. Like I said, what she is experiencing is not of this world. From what I know, that's where you come in." He smiled at her.

Liz smiled back, a big, bright smile. Maybe there was hope for her and Dr. Kendall, after all.

Walking back down the hall towards the direction of Lou's room, she was still smiling, although she was a little sad for Lou. She figured they were probably going to keep him in the hospital for a few more days. Angels people believed in. Hell was quite another subject. From the story Lou had told her, Liz was sure the doctors concluded that he had totally lost it. She thought it was very disappointing; how people thought that hell was one big joke. Man were they ever in for an unfortunate surprise.

As Liz was headed towards Room 519, she glanced in the rooms on either side. Most of the people in the rooms were lying motionless in their beds, but a few were struggling, yells of protest filling the air. Liz figured those were the ones where their medicine had worn off.

Finally, she arrived at Room 519 and walked in. Seeing her, Lou immediately brightened, smiling from ear to ear.

"I almost didn't expect you to come back", Lou said. "Especially with how I always ridiculed you about-"

"Stop", Liz said, holding up a hand while sitting down. "All that is in the past. We need to work on everything day by day now. That's how the Lord tells us to live."

"No, Liz, I really need to tell you I'm sorry." Lou raised himself up to a sitting position in his bed. "I really am sorry for not believing and making fun of your faith."

"Lou, it's OK." Liz smiled. Actually, it wasn't OK at first, but since he was willing to accept the Lord, it made everything alright now.

"Do they ever let you out of this room?" She asked.

Lou glanced over to his window where the shade was drawn. Noticing this, Liz got up and opened it. It was dark already, but at least he was able to see the street lights outside.

"Yeah, they did let me take a walk in the hall today. Tomorrow I might get to go outside or in the patient lounge down the hall."

"Oh", Liz replied. She would never say this to Lou, but she hoped that she never had to be a patient in this place.

"Did you get a chance to read the Bible?" She asked.

Lou's face flushed a little. "I'm embarrassed to say that I didn't, even after our talk yesterday", he said. "They kept coming in and checking on me and giving me all this medicine which makes my eyes blurry. And I've been so tired."

"I understand", Liz said as she opened the yellow envelope, but inside she was rolling her eyes. What other excuses was he going to come up with? Inside the envelope was a Bible in paperback along with a yellow highlighter. She placed both in Lou's hands.

"Here, so you'll have your own personal copy. I've highlighted and bookmarked the passages you need to read- especially John 3:16- how to be saved. You can highlight whatever other passages that interest you." She tried to keep it short. Didn't want to seem too pushy on the outset- that's what scared people away.

"Thanks, Liz, I'll try to read some later."

Where did all his zeal go? What happened to the scared man who would do whatever it took to stay out of the hell that tried to claim him? Was it the medicine talking? Or was it Satan and his minions placing second thoughts in his mind? She really hoped it wasn't that, but no matter, she would help him- just one day at a time.

She started to walk towards the door- visiting hours were almost over. She turned towards Lou. "Well, I guess I'll get going", she said.

Lou looked at her, a small bit of pleading in his eyes. "Can you try to come back tomorrow? I would like to talk about this Bible. I'm going to try to start reading it- I promise."

"I will try to come back tomorrow, Lou", she said, smiling. "In the meantime, if you start reading, I'd like you to start with the Psalms. And don't forget John 3:16. Good night, Lou."

"Good night, Liz. Be safe. Oh, I want to tell you take as much time as you need taking care of your sister."

"Thanks, Lou. I think I will take the rest of the week."

"That's fine. Be safe, Liz."

As Liz arrived out in the parking lot and settled into her car for the short drive home, she was smiling. Maybe Lou could be reached, after all. Her smile quickly turned to a grimace of fear however, as she looked upwards towards the hospital windows. Standing in one of the fifth floor windows, looking out at the parking lot, looking out at *her*, was a tall, dark figure.

In one of its bony hands it held a scythe.

* * * * * * * * * *

The autopsy now over, Joe and Frank sat across from each other in silence. Frank was behind his desk, Joe was in the visitor's chair next to it. All they could do was sit there and stare off into space, minds whirling.

Finally, Frank spoke. "Joe, I really don't know what to make of this. Never in my twenty-seven years as an M.E. have I ever encountered anything like this."

Joe knew this to be true. He knew Frank had seen it all, or at least thought he did. If even he didn't know what had happened to Doug, then it truly was a mystery.

"Well Frank, all I can say is maybe we'd better look at it as being something from beyond this world."

Frank leaned back in his chair a little, rubbing his chin and gazing at Joe. He never believed in anything beyond what he could see, hear and touch, but if he was honest with himself, well… he just didn't have any other explanation for it.

Finally, he spoke. "I just have one question", he said to Joe as he picked up a pen and started twirling it between his fingers. "What do I put down as the cause of death?"

* * * * * * * * *

Liz hobbled out into Alisa's kitchen rubbing her eyes. She was hardly able to see they were so bleary.

"Hey sleepyhead." Alisa handed her a cup of hot tea. She knew how much Liz hated the taste of coffee. Looking at her glassy eyes and tired face she asked, "Did you get any sleep at all?" Alisa had almost just gotten home herself. Dr. Kendall had decided to go ahead and release her late the night before.

"Not much", she replied, rubbing one eye. She had tossed and turned all night, worrying about that figure she saw in the hospital window. She just had a feeling that it was Lou's room the figure was standing in. Liz knew that Satan always attacked the most when someone was trying to get away from him and turn to the Lord. She was going to try to do as much as she could to keep Lou on the right path and get him to accept Christ. If it meant a showdown between her, the devil, and his minions then so be it. She was ready.

* * * * * * * *

Rob ran to his locker at the sound of the dismissal bell. He had just finished the last class of the day- science. They were starting to learn more about chemistry today, which he liked.

He flung open his locker door and threw his backpack in. He had already completed all of his homework for tonight, and didn't need to take any books home.

He ran back over to Kevin's locker to wait for him. Surely, he couldn't have left the school already.

"Hey man, what's up?" Kevin clapped Rob on the back as he walked around his side to open his locker.

"Hey Kevin, I need to talk to you for a bit. Can we walk home together?"

Kevin didn't think much of it. "Sure man, let's go." Kevin grabbed a couple of books out of his locker and shoved them in his pack.

Rob made some small talk, mostly about sports, until they were well beyond the school. He didn't want anyone to hear anything they had to talk about.

They were almost halfway home when Rob asked, "Can I ask you something?"

Still walking, Kevin looked at him and nodded his head. "I heard that you've been saying some things about me. Some things about what I do late at night."

Kevin stopped short and gazed at Rob. The look on his face said that he had been caught. Inside, he knew that Don had said something to Rob. It had to be Don. He didn't tell anyone else what he had discovered Rob was up to.

"Rob..." he started. He might as well own up to it, but it wasn't for the reason that Rob might think. "Look man, I didn't mean to follow you..."

"*Follow* me?" Rob raised his voice, his eyebrows knitting together in the beginning of anger.

Kevin stepped back a little, afraid that Rob was going to hit him. "To tell you the truth, I came over that night to talk to Lisa."

Lisa was Rob's seventeen-year-old sister and a junior at the high school they had both attended. Rob knew that Kevin had liked her for a very long time, possibly since they were in the sixth grade. He didn't think the feelings were mutual; however, Kevin never gave up.

"I came over to ask her if I could be her date for the junior prom. She said she'd think about it."

Rob was pretty sure Kevin was not the first guy to ask his sister to the prom. Pretty and popular, Lisa had long, flowing wavy brown hair with black highlights and bright green eyes. She was of average height, about five foot five, and had a small, athletic build. She could easily go into a store and grab anything off of the rack and have it look good on her.

She didn't seem to be too interested in dating, however. She just liked to hang out with her friends, both inside and outside of the church she attended. She even tried to get the rest of the family to go to church, if it was just one time, but to no avail. They didn't even attend on Christmas or Easter, which really disappointed her. Nevertheless, Lisa asked each family member if they would go with her before every time she went to leave. Maybe one of these days, they would wake up and make God the central part of their lives. Until then, she would just keep trying.

Kevin continued. "After she said she'd think about it, she told me good night and went back in the house. When I went to leave, that's when I saw you running from the back of the house. For some reason, I just felt that I had to follow you- I had this urge to see where you were going. I actually thought maybe there was a party going on that I didn't know about."

Rob shifted from one foot to the other. There was a party going on alright, but not the kind that Kevin would want to attend.

"When I first saw you standing by that car, I thought maybe you were talking to someone about the party and maybe I could hear where it was at. But then, I saw you smash the car's window in, and I just knew when I didn't see you run away that you weren't just trying to "get" someone."

Rob's eyes narrowed a little. "What did you do after that?"

"I slipped back the way I came, making sure you didn't see me, and then I ran home." He knew what Rob was going to say next, so he continued.

"I couldn't really believe what I saw- I just couldn't get over seeing you breaking in to a car. Don knew something was wrong, so I told him. He's the only one I said anything to- honest."

A small smile crept over Rob's face. It had a lot to do with the relief he felt right now. "Look man, I really appreciate this. You don't think Don will say anything about this, do you?"

Kevin started walking and Rob followed. "If he hasn't said anything by now, I am pretty sure he won't. You're not still doing it, are you?"

"No Kevin, I'm not. That night you saw me was the last night- ever." Rob's face was as serious as he felt.

"That's good to know", Kevin replied.

Rob thought so too. He was very relieved that no one else knew and was glad he decided to quit- before he was caught.

Kevin and Rob continued home in silence.

* * * * * * * *

Liz finished her waffles, washed her plate, and turned around to look at her big sister. Liz had been at her house four days now.

"Are you doing OK, Alisa?"

Alisa walked up to Liz and stood at her right side, smiling while she twirled some of Liz's bright blonde hair.

"I'm doing just fine, especially since you're here. It's always so peaceful when you're around."

Liz sighed inwardly as she sat down at the table and chair set in the kitchen. Alisa would not have to depend on her being there for peace if she would just accept Christ.

"I haven't slept this good in a long time- all thanks to you", Alisa said.

"I'm glad", Liz replied. "Although it's not from me."

Alisa rolled her eyes.

"I'll be here about three more days and then I've got to get back…" Liz trailed off as Jack walked into the room.

"Hey gorgeous." Jack slid his arms around Alisa's shoulders and planted a kiss on her lips. "I'm so glad you are doing better." He looked at Liz. "And how much longer is my favorite sister-in-law staying?"

"Three days", Liz replied, "Then I guess it's time to go back to work." She frowned at this last statement. She enjoyed her job- to a degree- and it paid well, but there was so much more she'd rather be doing. Something that really mattered. She was feeling led to start working for the Lord, but not enough to know exactly what it was yet.

She turned to Alisa. "Are you going to be OK for a little while?" Alisa had not seen the "figure" since she left the hospital. She was beginning to not mind staying by herself anymore although after a few conversations between Liz and her she was convinced that it was a demon that she had been seeing.

"Sure honey, where are you going?" Alisa was now rooting through the large stainless-steel refrigerator.

"I'm going to go back to the hospital to see Lou", Liz replied, grabbing her purse and car keys and heading for the front door. "I'll see you a little later."

"See you." Alisa's voice sounded muffled from within the refrigerator.

* * * * * *

Joe and Frank were just starting to wrap things up. It was now seven o'clock in the morning. Joe had no need to call Stella- being a wife to a cop, she knew better than to wait up- she just went to bed when she was tired, and prayed that God would protect him.

Frank was sitting as his desk deliberating what to write down as the cause of death, when he and Joe decided to take one more look at Doug's body. They wanted to make sure they covered each and every possible angle, not leaving any stone unturned. They both knew that what was written on Doug's death certificate could possibly affect his family for the rest of their lives, so they wanted to ensure it was as accurate as possible.

They thoroughly reviewed Doug's body for about three more hours, finally stopping at six a.m. Then, they both washed up and sat down in Frank's office, getting on the internet to research every possible cause of Doug's death. The only thing they found that was remotely close were some old medical journals depicting strange disappearances, and evidence of people who were taken after making "deals with the devil". In Frank's medical database, the death certificates on record were no help. The closest ones to this situation either stated "fire" or "unknown".

Frank wasn't quite sure what to do. In all his years as an M.E., he had *never* encountered anything like this. He thought he had seen it all until now. If he put "fire" on the certificate that wouldn't be true, even though Doug's insides appeared burnt up. There was no real fire. Natural causes were definitely out- this was *not* natural at *all*. The only thing he could do was go back to his original decision- put "unknown" on the certificate and answer any questions Doug's family might ask.

Frank placed the certificate in the typewriter behind his desk and started to type. He wanted to have this done and off to the family's personal doctor within the next hour or so. It had been a long night, which led into a long morning. None of this was unusual for himself or Joe. They were used to endless sleepless nights fading into the early morning hours.

Finally, Joe spoke. "Are you going with 'unknown' then?" He already knew the answer; he was just trying to confirm it by hearing it aloud from Frank.

"Yes, I'm going to have to", Frank replied as he finished with the typewriter.

"I'm going to head on out. Anything you need for me to do?"

"Yes, there is." Frank looked like he was in serious thought.

Joe gazed down at Frank as he stood across from his desk waiting to see what was needed.

"Just pray for Doug's family", Frank said matter-of-factly. He was not a religious man, but even he was beginning to think that there was a lot more to Doug's death than met the eye.

Seeing the surprised look on Joe's face, Frank added, "Yeah, Joe, that's about all we can do. There are going to be a lot of unanswered questions for this family, and they are going to need as much strength and comfort as they can get."

FIVE

Liz walked down the hallway of the fifth floor of North General Hospital for what she hoped would be one of her final times. She was getting to know this place pretty well, and she didn't really like it. Although, if it meant bumping into Dr. Kendall, then…

Arriving at Room 519, she stopped short. There was no one in the room. The bed was freshly made and there were no personal belongings lying around.

Her heart sank, which surprised her. It was a good thing that Lou was being released, wasn't it? Still, she just couldn't get the thought of that figure out of her mind. She knew that satan was going to be trying to get to Lou now that he was open to what the Lord had in store for his life. It was only a matter of time before he attacked Lou even more than ever. She had to make sure that he knew how to defend himself.

She walked back down the hall a little to the nurses' station, scanning the area for Dr. Kendall. He was nowhere near the area.

When she asked one of the nurses sitting at the station about Lou, the nurse confirmed that yes, he had been released about a half hour ago. Liz thanked her and walked back down the hall to take the stairs to the main floor and out of the hospital.

Upon reaching the landing of the fourth floor, she let out a small gasp as she saw Dr. Kendall coming up the stairs towards her.

"Hello, Liz", he said, smiling. She couldn't believe he remembered her name.

"Hello Dr. Kendall", she said.

He stopped at the fourth floor landing, standing directly in front of her. Was it her, or did he look extra good today?

"How is Alisa doing? Has she had any more 'visits'?"

"Alisa is doing pretty well. She doesn't seem to be as nervous at all, and I don't think she's seen anything else since she's been home."

"I am so glad to hear it", he said. He stood there for a while after that, just looking at Liz. She stared back, gazing into his bright blue eyes. He knew he could get in a lot of trouble for cornering her like he was doing. If it was any other woman he wouldn't be doing this, but something told him that Liz was not any other woman.

"Can I call you sometime?" He blurted out. He just couldn't stop himself- there was something about Liz that was drawing him to her.

"Dr. Kendall, you can call me anytime", Liz said, smiling.

"Good", he breathed. "Maybe we can go out soon."

"Maybe, soon." Liz was still smiling.

They looked at each other for a few more minutes. Liz wanted him to kiss her very badly, but she wanted her first kiss from Dr. David Kendall, M.D. to be perfect. A hospital stairwell was not it.

Liz reached in her purse, pulling out a piece of paper and a pen. After writing her number down, she then pressed the piece of paper in Dr. Kendall's hand. "Call me as soon as you can", she said.

"I will- talk to you soon", he said, walking away to go back up the stairs to the fifth floor. He never felt like this before; breathless and in a daze.

Once Liz heard the door close behind him, she flopped against the wall and sighed dreamily. She couldn't believe how fast things happened. She went from not thinking much about Dr. Kendall to getting ready to go out on a date with him. She was sure she would be on cloud nine the rest of the day.

She decided to continue down the staircase out of the hospital and go directly to Lou's house. She was sure that was where he would be at. If not, she could just leave him a note.

* * * * * * * * * * * * *

"I'll be back- I really have to go", Lou Steton yelled to a few of his waiting team mates as he was running to the woods. They were almost finished playing their last softball game of the evening, but he couldn't wait any longer. He was just released from the hospital that morning, but he wanted to join his team tonight to try to take his mind off things. He headed back to the middle of the woods where lots of trees and bushes were and he thought no one could see him if they tried. He unzipped his softball pants and looked around. There wasn't anyone else nearby, but it was a habit- you had to make sure no one was spying on you. He looked down at the bush in front of him as he zipped his pants back up. What a relief to be done.

Lou blinked fast a couple of times- he thought he saw something underneath of that bush.

His heart almost jumped out of his chest when all of a sudden, a horrible demonic face was staring back up at him from the ground in front of the bush.

"Hi, Lou", it said softly to him as it started to be more than just a face. Hands started to appear, and then arms, and it was then reaching, grabbing for him...

Lou went tearing out of the woods screaming, zipping up his pants as he went. His stunned teammates stared for a few seconds as he was running towards them, and then started to gather around him as he hurriedly packed up his things.

"Lou, what is it?" His team captain asked. He thought maybe it was a snake or something, at worst a dead body. You just never knew these days.

"I h-h-h-a-a-ve t-t-t-t-to g-g-g-g-go", Lou stammered.

"Lou, what was in the woods?" His captain asked again.

"Tim, I just have to go", he said, much calmer this time.

Get it together, Lou, he thought. *You just have to keep it together until you get to your car. You don't want to go back into the hospital.*

"I thought I saw something. It was probably just a snake. I'm sorry, I just need to go."

"OK- well thanks for coming out today. I think you'd just better get some rest", Tim said. "Are you going to be alright?"

There was something about the look on Lou's face that he did not like. It was something more than just being tired. His other teammates saw it too- concern was written all over their faces.

"Yeah, Tim, I'll be fine", Lou said as normally as he could. He grabbed his softball duffel bag and quickly walked to his small car. Meanwhile, Tim grabbed his car keys and started to pack up his own duffel, leaving someone else in charge of the rest of the game. He would wait until Lou left, and then he was going to follow him, wherever he was going.

Flopping behind the wheel, Lou rubbed his forehead. How long was this going to go on? How much longer would he have to endure these sightings until whatever it was finally got him?

Suddenly, a small shrill voice popped into his mind. *Do it, Lou,* it said. The voice had a high-pitched, tinny quality to it.

Do it, Lou, you know what you have to do, Lou. The high-pitched tinny voice cackled at this new-found rhyme.

Do it, Lou. DO IT. This time the voice was louder, deeper, more persistent. *DO IT!!!!* It now hissed.

Lou rubbed his forehead again and again as he was driving down the road; driving to his house.

You know what you have to do, Lou, Lou, you know what you have to do, the voice said again and again, cackling and cackling in between each sentence.

"STOP IT!! JUST STOP IT ALREADY!!" Lou screamed. If someone was next to him on the road, they probably would have thought he was completely crazy.

The further he went down the road, though, the more depressed he became. It was not a normal depression; it was a deep, dark veil of despair. He could not explain it, but he had a sudden urge to grab his handgun and shoot himself in the head with it when he got home. The more he drove, the more urgent that thought- *need* – became.

Finally, he arrived at home, pulling up into the driveway of his small, two-story rancher. The tinny, sneering voice was silent for now, but all he wanted to do was go into his bedroom and grab his gun. God, the Bible, the conversations with Liz- none of that even entered his mind right now- just an ever-widening chasm of gloom and sadness.

As he fumbled with the key in his front door, the voice started up again. "Do it, Lou, do it, Lou, you know what you have to do." The voice wasn't cackling this time. In fact, it was getting louder, more insistent, the voice itself getting deeper.

Finally, he was able to open the door and wade in. He felt like he was walking through mud. He didn't even bother to get his softball supplies out of his car- he wouldn't be needing them anymore. "Do it, Lou... Now, Lou- NOW!! Just get it over with, who cares if you live or die?" The voice was a little softer now, but still persistent.

He shook his head. All of his life, he never thought about suicide. Why now? Why all of a sudden? He had a quick answer come across his mind- it must be one of those "attacks" that Liz was always talking about.

Slowly, he walked towards his bedroom. It almost felt like he was on autopilot. Every ounce of his being did not want to go into his bedroom and grab that gun, but it was almost as if someone else was guiding him- pushing him- in that direction. His thoughts weren't even clear at this point- just a muddling of voices saying all kinds of things at the same time.

Finally, he arrived at his bedroom and opened up the nightstand that was next to the left side of his bed, by the window. Taking the gun out and holding it in his hand- *"Do it, Lou"*, the voice interjected- he thought, *What's the use? I am just going to be hounded by this being every day anyway, I might as well get it over with. I'm probably going to end up in and out of the loony bin the rest of my life.*

He sat down on the edge of his bed facing the window as he heard pounding on his front door.

"Lou? You in there? Hey LOU! Can you hear me?? Open up, man. I forgot to tell you something about the team." It was Tim.

Lou wanted to go and open the door, even though deep down he felt it was a trick, but something was not letting him do it. It felt like he was cemented to his bed. He laid the gun down next to him on the bed and tried to get up, and was violently pushed back down. Another wave of despair, and this time panic, overtook him. He had the sudden feeling that he must hurry up and do what he was led here to do, and it was now or never.

Lou picked the gun back up and placed it in his mouth, oblivious to the ever-insistent pounding on his front door.

Tears starting to stream down his face, he suddenly thought about his two children.

"Don't worry about them, Lou, they're teenagers now and they don't need you anymore. Your job is done."

The voice, which was deeper now and no longer tinny, had decided to chime in again. It continued, strangely starting to sound like his own voice. "No one cares anymore, Lou, no one cares. Sharon will be glad that you are gone, so she don't have to deal with you anymore."

Sharon was his ex-wife. They were on good terms, even though they only spoke when it had something to do with the kids.

BANG! was the last sound Lou heard as he pulled the trigger and fell backward on his bed, a red stain quickly spreading behind him.

Megan bypassed the elevator leading to her expansive basement and the wine cellar. She felt like taking the stairs tonight.

With Melanie safely tucked into bed and now sound asleep, Megan needed to find a little stress relief. She had been so short with Melanie since Doug's death, and it wasn't the little girl's fault. She was just missing her husband terribly, even though she mostly saw him only in the evenings. It was just having a man around the house to be there with her at night; protecting her, loving her...

She thought that Melanie and her would be more than OK financially, especially if she sold the house. Sure, she loved it, and she didn't want to move right away as it reminded her of Doug, but it was really way too big for just the two of them. Even though she had hired someone to keep it clean, it was just too big. And, she felt, too unsafe.

Walking into her wine cellar, she closed the solid wooden door behind her and flipped the light switch on. The ten by thirteen area held over two hundred and fifty different kinds of wine and still had plenty of room to spare. Megan was proud of this room: she had decorated it herself, even painting a mural of an Italian wine country-side on one of the walls. A Swarovski chandelier made a beautiful addition to the ceiling.

Grabbing one of the bottles of Chablis, Megan set it down on the table to the left side of the room as she crossed it to fetch a large wine glass and a corkscrew. Pulling the cork out, she poured herself a full glass and sat down before heading back upstairs.

Taking a huge drink, she relaxed a little in her padded leather chair, letting out a long, loud sigh. She really didn't like moving, but didn't want to wait until Melanie got too much older either, when friendships were harder to make.

She finished the rest of her wine on the second drink, immediately feeling the warm, relaxing feeling that comes with it. She got up, grabbed her bottle and glass, turned off the light and left the room, heading towards the elevator. She didn't want to take the risk of breaking anything and having all that glass to clean up.

Arriving upstairs on the second floor, she got out and walked slowly towards the kitchen. Preparing to sit down at the large glass and wooden table that was close to the island, she stopped and sniffed the air. She thought she detected a faint whiff of sewage.

"That's odd", she said to herself. There were no bathrooms close to the kitchen, and as far as she knew, the pipes in the walls weren't leaking, either.

As Megan was walking around the perimeter of the kitchen checking the walls for signs of leaking pipes anyway, the smell got stronger, assaulting her nose and causing a look of disgust to cross her face. She decided to pour herself another glass of wine. Maybe that would help it go away, especially if it was just her imagination.

Just as she was getting ready to grab the wine bottle for her second glass, she froze. There was a puddle of blood on the floor next to her kitchen island.

Her heart starting to pound, the different possibilities were whirling around in her mind. Her first thought was maybe Melanie came down into the kitchen and cut herself somehow. That was quickly dismissed, however, when she did not see any bloody footprints leading away from the puddle. Not only that, but Melanie would have tried to find her and would be yelling "Mom!" all over the house.

Her second thought was that maybe an animal or worse, an intruder had gotten into the house somehow. Or maybe it was someone who was hurt and had come in seeking help?

She got her answer quicker than she wanted as suddenly, a figure started rising out of the puddle. Megan wasn't relaxed at all anymore. Eyes wide, she couldn't make out any limbs, only that this figure was not human and that it was very tall; at least over six feet. The smell of sewage was almost overwhelming now.

Finally, the figure had completely risen out of the pool of blood and stood there before her. Its skin, or whatever it had that could pass for skin, was almost as red as the blood that surrounded its clawed feet. It had no hair, yellow eyes, deep grooves all over its face, and with its mouth partly open, Megan could see broken, rotted, yellow teeth.

She had to steady herself on the table behind her as a terrible realization hit home and she felt herself growing faint. She knew now. It was the ugly man. She remembered Melanie talking about him quite often but she was the only person who was able to see him. Megan guessed maybe he changed his mind.

"Hello, Megan", he said, in a low, gravelly voice.

Megan's jaw dropped open wide as she decided whether to make a run for it or reply to him. It didn't matter anyway. Legs locked in place, her feet were frozen to the floor.

"I have your Dougie here with me, Megan", he said, edging a little closer to her. "Want to see him? Better yet, want to come *be* with him?"

Megan fell down in the chair behind her trying to scream, but the only sounds that would come out of her mouth was a half-whimper.

The ugly man advanced towards her a couple of steps. Megan felt that she was going to die right then.

"See you soon, Megan dear", he said before disappearing back into the floor, the pool of blood vanishing in thin air.

Megan sat at her kitchen table for a very long time after that, legs shaking, mouth still open in stunned silence.

* * * * * * * * * * *

Rob hung up the phone after talking to Kim Simone, one of his longtime friends. She had always had a crush on him ever since they were in the sixth grade, but never really acted on it. She did, however, always try to come up with things for them to do, and today was no exception. She wanted him to join a paranormal group that she was starting.

Rob really didn't have an interest in the supernatural or the occult and he didn't really believe any of it either, but he thought he might give it a try. Kim just needed someone to set up and operate some of the equipment, and it would keep him busy and away from cars on weekend nights, anyway. It would also provide him with a little bit of spending money as they would charge a nominal fee for their investigations.

He grabbed his video camera and extra battery as well as some memory cards. Kim already had a voice recorder as well as a thermographic video camera. Two other people that were to be on the team had video cameras, voice recorders, and some other equipment. They were going to have their first investigation tomorrow, which Karen was not thrilled about. She was not religious, but she did not want to be involved with anything having to do with the supernatural or the occult, and that included Robbie messing with it as well.

In any case, Rob felt that he was on the right track. It would give him a fresh start from the life of crime that he was heading towards.

Epilogue

Joe and Stella walked down the steps of St. Mary's Catholic Church, looking up expectantly at the front door. Frank was still inside, talking to a couple of friends whom he hadn't seen around in about two weeks. All of them had started coming to church about eleven months ago- about a month after Doug died- and they hadn't missed a Sunday since.

Frank finally came out smiling. All three of them always felt better after spending time in the morning mass.

"So, what are you and Jenny going to do the rest of the day?" Joe asked him. Frank had met Jenny in church six months ago. She had been divorced for about nine years. Their relationship progressed from bible study friends, to friends, to dating, and now starting to get a little serious. They both did not feel the need to rush things- both age sixty-one, they felt that they still had plenty of time.

"I'm not sure. I think we may take a hike or something", Frank said with a grin. "We may even let the dogs tag along." Jenny loved the outdoors, and frequently took her two golden retrievers along when she hiked. When her and Frank started going out a bit more, she was able to convince him to come along as well. After he went the first time, he was hooked. He had never realized just how relaxing the outdoors was. It made him feel so *alive*. He was sure that Jenny had something to do with that too.

"What are you and Stella doing the rest of the day?" He asked, although he already knew the answer. Both of them did not believe in doing anything at all after church- just relaxing around the apartment, reading books and playing games.

"Well, we have a family party to go to today, actually", Stella replied. "One of our nieces is turning five."

"That's a good age. You two have a great time and I'll talk to you later in the week", he said.

"Alright, Frank, have a wonderful hike", Joe replied.

As Frank walked to his car, he knew he would. It was going to be one of many more wonderful hikes with Jenny to come.

* * * * * * * * * * * *

Rob walked into Kim's room, video camera clutched in one hand. They were going on an investigation later that evening, but Rob arrived at Kim's house a little early. He had been on this team for about a year now and really enjoyed it. He had not broken into any vehicles since, as his nights were mostly filled with investigations, going over evidence, and other related things.

Rob arrived early at Kim's because he wanted to learn a little more about this "wicca" that she had been talking about. She had been practicing it for the past five months and spoke to Rob about it often- telling him what kind of spells she was doing and the results. She claimed that things were so much better for her since she got involved in it, which piqued Rob's curiosity. After all, they were coming up on their senior year and they didn't have too much time until they were out in the "real" world. It was never too early to plan for the future.

He wanted to see Kim perform one of her spells and get her to tell him more about her "religion". She also started performing a blessing ritual, asking the gods to place a circle of protection around them before they went on their investigations.

"Hey Robby", Kim said with a big smile as she looked up at him. She was kneeling within a pentacle rug she had laid down in the middle of the floor. At each point, she had placed a white pillar candle and was preparing to light them.

"You're just in time", she said. "I was getting ready to do our protection ritual."

"OK", Rob said as he sat down on the edge of her bed, preparing to watch.

Kim leaned forward towards each candle, lighting one at a time. She then got up and closed the blinds to both of the windows in her room to make it as dark as possible on this bright mid-June day.

Coming back towards the bed, she sat down next to Rob. "This will be one of many rituals I will show you", she said as she stared into his dark brown eyes. "I want you to see how good wicca has been to me", she whispered.

"I can't wait to learn all of this from you", Rob said, looking deep into Kim's light brown eyes. He leaned closer to kiss her, putting an arm around her shoulder.

Kim was more than glad to reciprocate. This was a moment she had been waiting on for a very long time. She leaned into Rob, encircling both of her arms around his waist. The only thing was, what about Karen?!

Rob must have thought the same thing too, because he abruptly broke the kiss.

"I- I'm sorry", he half-whispered. "I…"

Kim stood up. "It's OK", she said. "It's my fault. I know that you are not going to leave Karen, least of all for me. You love her. She or no one else needs to know about what happened."

Kim looked at him sincerely. She meant every word that she said. Of course she wanted Rob, but she knew that would never happen as long as he loved Karen. She was just not the type of girl who would stand in the way or try to break a relationship up.

"I appreciate that, Kim. Again, I'm sorry", Rob replied.

"Say no more. There is really nothing to be sorry about", she said. This kiss would stay with Kim for a long time to come, maybe even the rest of her life.

Kim stood up to get a ritual book out of one of her dresser drawers.

"Well, let's get this started", she said. "Then, I'll tell you about some things that have happened."

"Sounds good", Rob said. He took out a pad of paper and a pen to prepare to take notes and write the ritual down. He was looking forward to getting more involved in wicca as time went on.

* * * * * * * * * * *

Megan shielded her eyes from the sun, straining to see Melanie out on the soccer field. She had her sunglasses on, but the midday summer sun was extremely bright. It didn't help that her eyes were bleary from drinking heavily the night before.

Her alcohol habit had started taking its toll on her once youthful face. Her normally bright complexion was starting to show signs of ruddy dullness. Wrinkles were starting to appear around her eyes, mouth and forehead.

Her outward appearance wasn't the only thing that it was affecting, either. Most mornings, she could barely get out of bed; either exhausted from being up all night due to being too scared to sleep, or unable to function with a raging hangover.

Earlier that year, she had decided to sell the house. Frankly, she was afraid to stay there; afraid that the ugly man would keep coming back. Doug had left behind plenty of money, but Megan just could not stand to stay in that house any longer.

With the money from Doug and the sale of the house, she bought a much cozier one and put the rest in the bank. She also thought it would be a good idea to hire a nanny; at least for the mornings and evenings. Most mornings, she was not able to get Melanie off to school, and most evenings her drinking started right after supper, rendering her too helpless to assist Melanie with her homework and get her ready for bed, even though Melanie was seven years old now and could do a lot of that herself.

The drinking seemed to be the only thing that kept Megan sane, even though she knew she eventually had to stop. The nanny she hired was good, but she didn't want someone else raising her daughter. Not only that, but she also had to hire a housekeeper most of the time to clean her small house which she should have been easily able to manage on her own.

She had not seen the ugly man again after his appearance to her in the house which she and Doug had once shared. Maybe she had drank him into oblivion, somehow. That fact did nothing to relieve Megan, however. She was constantly on edge; continually worrying if he was going to come back and take her with him. It had actually started to take its toll on her entire life to include her relationship with Melanie. She would snap at her for no reason- the stress of constantly being paralyzed in fear eating away at her.

That's when she took up drinking. She wasn't living life anyway, but at least when she drank she wasn't worrying about the ugly man coming to claim her.

This morning when she woke up, head aching as usual, she decided she was going to start cutting back on her drinking for Melanie's sake. If she had to, she would go talk to someone to help see her through this. She didn't want to talk to Melanie, even though she knew Melanie had seen the ugly man many times before. Melanie had pulled through the agony of her father's death very well to Megan's relief, and she didn't want to dredge up any dormant bad memories or thoughts that maybe her daddy wasn't in heaven, after all.

"Go, Melanie!" Megan stood up and yelled across the field. She was finally able to see her, and she was preparing to score a goal. She was doing really well playing the game and enjoyed it very much.

"Yes! GO, MELANIE!!" Melanie made the goal, her teammates congratulating her and clapping her on the back. Megan clapped her hands as well, laughing.

It felt good for her to be out after all this time. This was the first time she was really able to enjoy herself after Doug's death.

Maybe this was the first step towards her sobriety, after all. Only time would tell. If not, the ugly man would win, imprisoning Megan in a sea of fear, and alcohol.

* * * * * * * * * *

Liz had just finished having lunch with Alisa at her house and was relaxing in a recliner in Alisa's family room before getting ready to go home and then out on another date with Dr. David Kendall, M.D. They had been dating pretty regular for almost a year now and Liz couldn't be happier. Her life was starting to take shape.

Alisa had told her to just take it easy while she took care of cleaning up. No one could ever do quite as good of a job cleaning up in Alisa's house in Alisa's eyes. Liz was glad to oblige- she *was* a little tired today. She had recently started taking demonology classes at her local church as well as doing a lot of at-home and on-line studying and as a consequence, there were a lot of late nights, of which David understood all too well. Now at twenty-five, she finally knew what the Lord had called her to do- through Him, she was to deliver people from the bonds of Satan. She knew that the Lord would set her up with who she needed to work with when her classes were completed. She knew that her work had only just begun, but He had been preparing her for it all along.

She wasn't sure if David was going to be supportive at first; after all, it was not really a calling that people talked about. He surprised her though by telling her that he supported her in whatever it was that she decided to do.

In the meantime, Liz was very proud of Alisa. She had survived her ordeal a lot better than most, and according to her, she had Liz to thank. Liz told her often that it was because she prayed for her all the time- the Lord had given her the strength to not let the demonic attacks scar her for life.

Not that what happened wouldn't stay with her for life, to be sure. It had been one year and Alisa still had flashbacks and nightmares about the demonic entity that had plagued her for a time. It took her a while to understand just what it was in the very beginning. Only after telling Liz everything that was going on was she able to know that it was, in fact, a demon and not a ghost like she originally thought. Liz took a lot of time to explain to her about what demons looked like (in their true form), how they behaved, and yes they could and would hurt you. This last thing scared Alisa half to death, but Liz assured her it did not have to be that way. If she would just accept Jesus as her savior, she would have His protection; the power of His cleansing blood would keep her safe and the demons at bay- if she believed of course.

Alisa told Liz every time she brought it up that she needed time to think about it to which Liz would respond: "Don't take too long." Liz would always come away wondering what the holdup was- just how much more convincing would she need? What else needed to happen before she was no longer able to make the most important decision of her life- the decision of where she would spend eternity? She would then start to worry that if Alisa did not accept Christ now, she never would.

Jack wasn't any better, either. Yes, this had happened to his wife- someone close to him, so you'd think he'd be a little convinced, right? Wrong. Jack wasn't any closer to believing in God then he was before, to which Liz would wonder just how did he think everything got here on the earth, including him? Whenever she asked, he didn't have much of an answer. It was usually along the lines of "It just appeared." Liz would then respond, "That's right, it just appeared because God created it." Jack would never have anything else to say after that, but you could tell he was thinking about it real hard.

Liz couldn't allow herself to worry about them- it was all in God's hands. Worry was a tool of the devil and she couldn't allow herself to be caught in one of his traps. The Holy Spirit would reach them- all in good time. Until then, the Lord would use her to convict their hearts and minds a little more.

As Liz kissed her sister goodbye and headed to her car for the short drive home, her thoughts turned to Lou as they often did.

It took Liz a long time to get over Lou's death and how she felt was a huge failure on her part. First Denni, then Richard, now Lou. If one of her duties was to help lead people to Christ, she was failing miserably. She felt like she let them all down and it called for a lot of nights bitterly crying herself to sleep. She was just able to get to Lou; to show him how to be saved, and then satan ripped him away, snatching God's truth out of the grip of his understanding.

Liz was in a deep numbing shock for a long, long time after Lou's death. She did a lot of sleeping too, finally coming out of her funk after a lot of praying for deliverance from one of the enemy's attacks. She just couldn't help but question why Lou did what he did. He was doing so well, or so she thought. He was willing to hear what she had to say; willing to accept Christ, and then he went and killed himself. It all happened so fast, Liz was convinced that it was nothing but the handiwork of the enemy.

She wiped the tears from her eyes as she opened the front door of her house and stepped inside. Richard was another soul who was lost forever; another one who was ripped away by satan before he had a chance to accept the Lord. Same way with Denni.

Liz sighed heavily as she flopped on her living room couch, head in her hands. She knew that there were going to be setbacks as well as victories in what she felt she was being called to do, but every soul who was lost… well, that was just unacceptable. She was just going to have to modify her tactics; to try to be more aggressive without pushing people further away. It was her duty to try to reach as many souls as possible.

After all, time was getting short and the enemy was ramping up his efforts- doing whatever it took to discourage people from following the Lord. From what Liz could see, he was pretty successful at it, too.

Liz tried not to dwell on it too much or allow herself to get depressed about it, as she realized that was another one of the enemy's tactics. If she allowed herself to get discouraged- to lose faith- and then give up, well, she would just be another person who would have stepped aside out of satan's way.

Liz was determined not to let that happen. She had to clothe herself in Jesus' armor every minute of the day so she could always be defended against the enemy's attacks and be able to perform the work that the Lord had called her to do.

Little did Liz know as she prepared to make her tea and read the Bible for a while that this was only the beginning of the attacks that were to come.

END

www.ingramcontent.com/pod-product-compliance
Lightning Source LLC
Chambersburg PA
CBHW021124130626
46554CB00002B/849